Cracked Classics

Crack open all the books in

Cracked Classics

Cracked Classics

Dracula

Trapped in Transylvania

By Tony Abbott

Hyperion
New York

Text copyright © 2002 by Tony Abbott
Cracked Classics, Volo, and the Volo colophon are trademarks of Disney Enterprises, Inc.
Cover illustration by Gris Grimly

Printed in the United States of America
First Edition
1 3 5 7 9 10 8 6 4 2
This book is set in 11.5-pt. Cheltenham.

ISBN 0-7868-1324-5
Visit www.volobooks.com

Chapter 1

"Blah, blah, mumble, mumble," somebody was saying. "Mumble, mumble, blah, blah, blah . . ."

It was first thing Monday morning in Mr. Wexler's English class. I was feeling all bright and fresh after sleeping through the weekend.

Behind me sat my best-friend-for-life-even-though-she's-a-girl: Francine—Frankie—Lang.

"Blah, blah," the voice went on, which was making me sleepy all over again. To keep myself awake, I turned around.

"Hey, Frankie," I whispered.

"Hey, Devin," she whispered back.

I admire Frankie very much, and now she was proving why by doing two things at once. First, she was tugging on her hair. Second, she was staring at the ceiling.

"Wanna catch some tube time in the AV room between classes?" I asked.

She flicked her eyes down to me. "Sure, what's on?"

"Does it matter?"

"No," she chuckled. "Anything's better than English class."

I was just about to agree, when that distant talking suddenly got louder.

"Blah, blah, mumble, mumble . . . Devin and Frankie!"

I froze. Frankie froze. We were caught. Again.

"Stand up, you two!" Mr. Wexler said, storming down the aisle and screeching to a halt at our desks.

When we stood up, he frowned deeply at us. As he frowned, his eyebrows, which were so close and so thick, turned into one long bushy hedge.

"You haven't been listening to a single word I've been saying, have you?" he said, his voice all snarly. "You think this is playtime for you, don't you? Do you think school is just one big joke? Why do you even come to class if you're not going to listen? Have you ever tried to learn anything?"

"If this a quiz," said Frankie, "I'm pretty sure I suddenly need to go to the nurse."

I raised my hand. "The answers are: yes, no, sometimes, our parents make us, and once a long time ago but it didn't work."

Mr. Wexler's nose was this little button just big enough to keep his glasses from falling into his teeth. Right now the nose was turning bright red.

"The sad thing is, you two don't even bother to apply yourselves!" he said. "Neither of you is living up to your potential!"

"I'm due for a growth spurt soon," said Frankie.

"Oh, yes!" Mr. Wexler said, oozing a fake smile. "So funny. The king and queen of the smart comeback."

"Let me get this straight," said Frankie. "You want us to come back when we're smart?"

"And you think I'm a king?" I asked.

Mr. Wexler's single bushy eyebrow wriggled.

"Please just take your seats and wait here!" He hustled back to his own desk.

Frankie turned to me. "Where are we supposed to take our seats if we have to wait here?"

I shrugged. "Teachers speak a different language."

At least it seemed so to Frankie and me.

You see, we aren't what you call the best students in the sixth grade at Palmdale Middle School. In fact, some people might say Frankie and I are nowhere near the best. We're probably somewhere in the middle.

Maybe lower middle. Okay, middle lower.

Everybody says we don't do great in school because we don't read. But we do read! Lots.

Okay, a little.

Fine, we don't read. But it's only because we have lots of our own stuff to do and it takes up every second of our time. People keep trying to wreck it, though. They make these big fat books just so that teachers like Mr. Wexler will have something to teach.

But for me and Frankie, it's like—why read when there's so much other stuff to do?

Anyway, more later. Here comes Mr. Wexler.

"Since you two are such *classic* cases of not applying yourselves," Mr. Wexler said as he walked toward us, "here's a real *classic* for you—"

Wham! Wham!

He dropped a thick book on each of our desks. "You don't like paying attention in class? Okay, I've got some homework for you. You will read this big classic book and you will give an oral report—both of you—in front of the whole class—tomorrow! You'll discuss plot, character, setting, and theme. And maybe, just maybe, I won't call your parents! And remember—read the whole book! That means every word!"

At that moment, the bell rang and we bounced out into the bustling school hall with everyone else.

"Frankie, it's bogus," I said, trying to hold the big

fat classic book in one hand as we tramped to our lockers.

"That thing hanging from your nose?" she said. "I think it's pronounced *booger*."

I rubbed it off. "No. It's bogus that we have to read this superlong chubby book. Look at it. It's full of pages from beginning to end. Not only that. There's printing on every single one of them!"

"What's the bad evil thing called?" she asked.

"D . . . R . . . A . . . *Dracula*?" I said. "That can't be right. *Dracula* is a movie."

"Some book. Doesn't even know what it is."

Frankie looked so glum her hair drooped. I hate that. I like when she's just happy and fun. But Frankie is very sensitive to sad stuff and I try to notice it and make her feel better. Just then, an idea came to me.

"Hey, Frankie, how about you come over to my house after supper? Maybe if we work together there's some kind of shortcut we can find. One head is better than two, right?"

"That's what they say," she said, finally smiling again. "You know, Devin, I never told you this, but sometimes, I like how you think. If that's what it's called."

I slapped her five, and we agreed to meet at my house after supper for a mondo cram session at 6:30.

At 7:48 sharp she showed up.

Chapter 2

"You're late for our mondo cram session," I said as Frankie stumbled in through the window of my little upstairs room. Frankie always climbs a tree to get in.

"I had to do stuff," she said, a little yawn seeping out of the corner of her mouth.

"Like what?"

"Well, first I had to think about coming over here. Then, I had to, you know, actually *come* over here. So that's two things. Stuff like that takes time to work out."

I nodded. "I hear you. Life's brutal that way."

She dumped her copy of the chubby book on my floor and lay down next to it. "So, do we have to start working right away or can we take a break first?"

"I'm not into torture!" I said. I closed the door and stacked her book and mine squarely against it to keep it closed. "This is a long, thick, and heavily chubby book," I said. "We have to work ourselves up to it. We have to *prepare*."

Frankie cracked a grin. "Okay, let's *prepare*!"

Here's a list of the stuff we did to prepare.

1. I fluffed the pillows before I stretched out on my bed. They needed lots of fluffing. Fifteen minutes.

2. I shot hoops, using my dirty socks as the ball and my hamper as the basket. Score: six socks, eighteen points (from the bed each basket is a three-pointer). For some reason, Frankie didn't play, even after I offered her a choice of right or left sock. Twelve minutes.

3. We couldn't start working until we found what smelled under my bed. We couldn't find it. I think it moved to the closet. Frankie said no way was she looking in my closet. She calls it "the Black Hole of Palmdale." Almost an hour.

4. To get our thumbs in shape for reading, we both tried to tear a deck of cards in half. The cards didn't tear, but I did hurt my thumbs. Then we played cards until my thumbs felt better. Forty-five minutes.

5. Frankie painted her toenails and fingernails pearly white. Bored with watching her, I did my left thumbnail with a red marker, then found it wouldn't

wash off, even after repeated rubbings. Cool. Thirty-two minutes.

6. When we were almost nearly ready to begin to start making notes on the chubby book, Frankie sharpened our pencil with my dad's electric sharpener. But she totally got into it. Soon only the eraser was left. Of course we had to find another pencil. Twenty-six minutes.

7. We had to rest after the search for a second pencil so we flipped around on the TV to see if anything good was on. That's when I knew we had luck on our side.

"Dracula!" I yelped. "It's actually on. The movie!"

"The movie of the chubby book?" said Frankie.

"*And,* the movie of our report!" I said. "Frankie, we're golden!" I refluffed my pillows and got into position.

The next thing I remember, the window was open, Frankie was gone, the sun was up, and my mom was banging pots in the hall to make me open my door because it was jammed shut by two fat chubby books.

"Uh-oh," I mumbled, rubbing my eyes. "D-Day."

A half hour later, lugging the books with me, I caught up with Frankie in the hall outside Mr. Wexler's class.

"Where did you go last night?" I asked her.

"It was this morning," she said. "And I went home

to sleep. I was so exhausted from all our preparing."

"But you saw the *Dracula* movie, right?"

She made a face. "No, did you?"

I made the same face. "Frankie, when I said we were golden, I was only half right. We're golden brown. Totally toasted."

And we were. As soon as we stepped into the classroom, Mr. Wexler bounced up from his desk.

"Ah! Our guests of honor have arrived," he cried gleefully. "Devin and Frankie, we're all waiting to hear about that great classic work of literature, *Dracula*. You may begin your *fabulous* oral report anytime. Now would be a fine time."

Frankie and I stood shivering at the front of the room.

"I only know one thing about Dracula," I whispered to her. "That he's a vampire."

"A guy that bites other people?" she whispered.

"Whoa! That's two things we know!" I said. "Hey, maybe we're golden again. I'm thinking if we can stretch out the report maybe we'll bluff our way through it and get straight As!"

"Or at least not fail," said Frankie.

"At least," I said.

"Now stop stalling, you two," Mr. Wexler said. "Please begin with a few words about the theme of the book."

We did rock, paper, scissors, and I won.

Frankie gave out a deep groan.

"*Dracula*'s theme . . ." she began, "is very compli-cated. I say this because *Dracula* is not only the name *of* the book, it's also the name of a person *in* the book!"

"Excellent on the theme, Frankie," I said, nodding thoughtfully. "Does anybody have any questions?"

No one did. But Mr. Wexler started mumbling something and rubbing his forehead.

"Dracula is an interesting character," he said. "We've been discussing character in class for the last two weeks, so please tell us what he is like."

I took a shot at that. "Dracula is quite a character. In many chapters you hear people saying, 'Hey, Dracula, you're quite a character.' And you know what? He is!"

"Good one!" Frankie slapped me five. "Our work here is nearly done!"

Mr. Wexler grumbled loudly. "Forget character. Tell us about the plot. Can you summarize the plot?"

Frankie shook her head. "I can't."

"Aha!" Mr. Wexler chirped. "You can't because you didn't read the book—"

"I can't summarize the plot," Frankie said, "because it doesn't happen in summer. It happens in winter."

Laughter erupted in the class.

Mr. Wexler breathed deeply as if trying to calm down. "Yes, well, let's move on to the setting of the story, shall we? We've been talking about setting in class—not that you two would know. So . . . where does the story take place?"

I jumped. "The whole story takes place . . ."

"Yes?" Mr. Wexler said.

"In a book!"

Frankie clapped. "Stick a fork in us—we are done!"

We started happily back to our seats.

"STOP!" Mr. Wexler screamed. His single eyebrow rolled like a caterpillar across his forehead. His face turned a shade of purple I'd never seen before. And weird little veins popped out all over his neck and head.

"You . . . you . . . you!" he sputtered.

"Us . . . us . . . us?" I replied.

"You . . . didn't read this book!" he said. "You don't know anything about this book. In fact, you don't know anything about *any* book! And I can't take it anymore! Maybe you should start spending more time around books. I'm sending you both to the library."

Frankie clutched her throat then clutched me. "The library? Where all the b-b-books are?"

Mr. Wexler nodded with a kind of crazed delight. "And the librarian will make you learn to love every single one of them."

"The librarian?" I mumbled. "Not . . ."

"Mrs. Figglehopper!" he said. "She'll teach you to respect books!"

"I've heard about her," I said. "She loves books so much it's scary."

Mr. Wexler was rocking slowly on his feet now. "Yes, by golly, Mrs. Figglehopper's just the one for you two! You'll be *different* after visiting her."

"That doesn't sound good," Frankie whispered.

"It sounds bad," I said.

"Go!" yelled our teacher. "To the library! Right away. GO-GO-GO!"

In less time than it takes to sneeze, Frankie and I were in the hall and on our way to the library.

Chapter 3

We wound through the school hallways, taking the longest way possible.

"We passed the library five times already," said Frankie. "Care to make it an even hundred?"

I sighed a deep sigh. "It's no use, Frankie. We'd just get caught, and it would be worse. Besides, we'd run out of life trying to dodge our fate. Let's get it over with."

I pushed open the double doors. We stepped in.

"Welcome to the library!" chirped a woman who was standing behind a long curving counter near the doors.

She was somewhere between the age of my mother and the age of my grandmother. She wore a dress with big flowers all over it. Her hair was all up in the back and had streaks of gray in it.

A sign on the counter next to her said CHECKOUT.

"Hello, Mrs. Checkout," I said. "We're here to see Mrs. Figglehopper, the library lady."

"I'm Mrs. Figglehopper, the librarian," the woman said. "And you must be Frankie and Devin."

Frankie staggered back. "She knows about us already! Life is closing in on us, Devin!"

"I won't go down without a fight," I squeaked.

"Follow me," Mrs. Figglehopper said. "I want to show you where you'll be working."

"Working?" I shot a fearful glance at Frankie.

"I know, dude," she said. "It's happening so fast."

In two quick moves, Mrs. Figglehopper brought us to a room marked WORKROOM.

"I don't like the sound of that," I whispered.

It was a small room with two tables set against one wall. They were stacked with crumbly old books.

Next to the tables was a desk with a computer. Beside it were boxes filled with all kinds of library junk.

"What are those?" I asked, pointing to something set against the back wall of the room. It looked like a doorway with no top. The sides were about four feet high.

"Security gates," Mrs. Figglehopper said. "But I like to call them zapper gates, from the sound they make—"

"The sound they make when you put innocent kids in them?" Frankie asked.

The librarian gave a little smile. "No. Libraries use security gates to stop people from removing books without checking them out."

"People actually steal books?" said Frankie.

"Some people will do anything to read," Mrs. Figglehopper said, giving us a strange look. "Just as some will do anything not to read."

"Talk about reading," I said. "It's like she's reading my mind!"

"Check it out," Frankie whispered. "I'm keeping mine blank."

"Never mind the zapper gates," the lady went on. "They are cracked and don't work right. Here's what I want to show you. . . ."

She waved her hand at what filled up most of the rest of the room. Shelves and shelves and stacks and stacks of old books. Some had covers that were cracked. Some had pages that were ripped or falling out.

"They look like they belong in a museum," I said.

Frankie chugged a short laugh. "Or a graveyard! Some of those books look pretty dead."

"That's why I want you to help me bring them back to life," said Mrs. Figglehopper with a rumbly little chuckle. "I want you to help me repair them. These stacks hold the great classics of literature. They are very special works that people have read and reread for years. Little by little I'm fixing them so they can go back in the library where they belong. And you're going to help me."

"Us?" I said. "You want us to actually handle books?"

"We don't know anything about books," said Frankie. "Just ask Mr. Wexler."

The library lady nodded. "I think as you repair them, you will find that they are so interesting, you will want to read them. Wonderful worlds will open up to you. Your imagination will be enriched. Then maybe you will have more fun learning in Mr. Wexler's class. He's really a very good teacher, you know."

I looked at Frankie. "Why does it feel like everyone's plotting against us?"

The lady chuckled again. "You'll learn lots about plots in this room. And the sooner we get started, the sooner you'll discover how terrific books are—so let's begin!"

She took one book and showed us how to clear away the old smelly glue that was all crusted inside the cover. Then she put on some new smelly glue into what she called the "spine" of the book. That's the outside part between the front and back covers.

Then she showed us how to tape ripped pages using a special kind of tape. The tape also had a funny smell.

"Now I'd like you two to try fixing a book. How about this one?" She handed us a thick book with a crusty brown cover. It had gold letters on the front.

"D . . . R . . . A . . ." Frankie let out a screech. "*Dracula?* That's the book that sent us here! Oh, I'm having a heart attack. Call the ER!"

"*Dracula* is a good book," the librarian said, "a classic book written in 1897 by an Irish author named Bram Stoker. As you can see, this copy has gotten lots of use over the years. Now, I'll be back in forty minutes, just before the period is over. When I do, I hope to see you enjoying your work!"

She trundled off between the stacks. I heard the door squeak once, then shut.

"This is the pits," I mumbled.

"I find myself in total agreement," said Frankie. "But we'd better do what the library lady says. Or who knows what we'll end up doing!"

I shuddered at the thought. Frankie was right.

Carefully, I opened *Dracula*. The book wasn't in too bad shape. Mostly it had ripped pages.

Frankie tucked her stray hairs behind her ears

17

and pulled out a piece of the smelly tape. I found the first torn page and applied the tape.

"Cool," I said. "I repair old books."

I flipped through to find the next torn page. Frankie taped the rip on that one. "Me, also," she said.

Then we came to a picture.

"Whoa!" I said. "Classics illustrated!"

It was a drawing of a wagon, sort of like an old carriage. It was racing along a road between bunches of mountains and forests. Four horses attached to the front of the carriage were going all crazy and wild.

The scene was gloomy and shadowy and dark. Big clouds were tearing across the sky. It was spooky.

"What's that printing at the bottom of the picture?" Frankie asked, looking over my shoulder.

"Probably just some words," I said.

"What do they say?"

I turned to her. "You want me to read them?"

She gave me a look. "Duh."

I read, "'The coach . . . swayed . . . like . . . a boat . . . tossed on a stormy sea.'

"Hey, I told you I wasn't good at it."

"Wow!" said Frankie. "It does look like that! Those words work pretty good. What else does it say?"

"No way," I said, pushing the book in front of her. "I've read enough. You read."

"Nuh-uh," she said, shoving it back. "You do it."

I pushed the book. "No, you!"

"No, you!"

"No way!"

"Yes!"

"No!"

"Oops . . ."

The book went sailing out of our hands, over the stacks, and down toward the back of the room.

It fell right between those old zapper gates.

Kkkk—boom! There was a sudden flash of light and a quick, loud, booming sound.

Then a cloud of smoke puffed up from nowhere and billowed through the room.

"I can't see!" Frankie screamed.

Chapter 4

"Well, okay, I can see," Frankie said. "But it's all purple and blotchy in front of my eyes, like when someone snaps your picture and you end up with those spooky red eyes staring back out at everybody!"

"I know what you mean," I said. "But even more important—what just happened?"

I crept over to the gates, waving the smoke as I went.

The gates were glowing with a weird blue color.

"Did you break the gates?" said Frankie, creeping over next to me. "You broke them! Oh, dude!"

"Me?" I said. "You threw the book—"

"No, you!" she said. "Anyway, where did it go?"

I couldn't see the book. It wasn't behind the gates.

It wasn't on the floor. It wasn't anywhere.

But something else was.

A crack had opened in the back wall of the workroom, right behind the zapper gates. It was from the crack that all the smoke was pouring.

"I never saw that before," Frankie said. "Did you?"

I shook my head. "The big bang must have caused it, and that's where the book went to. Go get it, okay?"

"I'm not crawling around inside a wall!" she snapped. "Things might be living in there."

"Okay, okay," I said. "We both go. Ready . . . now!"

We slid in through the crack.

It was dark inside the wall, except for a bit of light coming from somewhere ahead of us. I stepped toward it and felt cool air rushing over us.

"I think we're heading out of the building," I said.

"That makes no sense. We should be hitting the janitor's supply closet any time now. Hey, there's the book." Frankie picked up the copy of *Dracula* from the ground.

I stopped. It was still smoky around me, but I realized that the ground was rough beneath my feet.

"You found the book," I said. "But where are we?"

Frankie peered ahead, squinting. I did, too.

"Whoaaaa . . ."

We were on a road. A dirt road. And all around us were forests and steep hills.

Plus it was dark, as if it were the end of the day.

"This is all wrong," said Frankie. "If we're outside, we should be able to see the parking lot. Besides, it's a sunny day. But I see no cars and no sun."

"We'd better get back to the workroom before somebody says we broke the library," I said.

But when we turned around, the bright blue light from the zapper gates was nowhere, and the crack in the wall was gone. In their place were just more woods and road stretching into the distance.

"This is so not good," I mumbled.

"It's so not possible, either!" said Frankie. "Unless . . . Devin! What if we're dead! What if the zapper gates blew us up big time and we're dead? And this is, you know, heaven!"

"Then where are the tables of food and the big TVs?"

Frankie thought about that. "Okay, so it's not heaven. But it does look sort of familiar."

Then it hit me. "Of course it looks familiar! It's just like . . . like . . . like . . . whoa!"

I grabbed the book from her and flipped it open. "It's—this!" I showed her the picture of the dirt road with mountains on both sides and forests all around. It was creepy and gloomy and shadowy and dark. Big black clouds were racing across the sky.

I looked up.

Big black clouds *were* racing across the sky.

"Whoa and double whoa!" said Frankie. "The only thing different is that there's a carriage in the picture—"

That's when we heard hooves pounding on the road.

We whirled around, and there it was—a carriage with four wild horses tearing down the road right at us. The wheels were squeaking and squealing. The carriage was bouncing. Exactly like in the picture.

"Just like a boat on a stormy sea!" Frankie gasped. "Devin, you know what this means? We're—"

"I know!" I said. "We're not in school anymore!"

"No, it means we're—"

"In big trouble!"

"No, we're—"

"Probably going to die!"

"WILL YOU LET ME FINISH!" Frankie yelled. "It means—we're in the book!"

She grabbed the book from me and shook it in my face. "We're in . . . *DRACULA!*"

Chapter 5

We were just about to dive into the bushes when—
errrrch!—the carriage driver pulled on the reins and
the horses screeched to a nasty stop.

A moment later, the carriage door swung open.

Nobody came out.

Nobody said, "Hi!"

Nobody said, "Get back to the library!"

Nothing.

It was just the carriage door swinging on its
hinges and the horses snorting noisily.

I looked at Frankie. "Okay, pal. Options?"

"I don't see any," she said. "I mean, look around."

I did. Dark night. Dark sky. Dark clouds. Dark
woods. Not a Palmdale Middle School in sight.

"You've got a point," I said.

We hopped in the carriage.

As soon as we did, the driver cracked his whip and the carriage jerked away, sending us crashing onto the seat next to a man dressed in a suit. He looked a little younger than my dad, had curly brown hair, and seemed more or less fairly normal.

On the seat across from us were two extremely old people who I think were women. Their faces were all pruney with wrinkles and they appeared to be wearing everything they owned.

"The layered look must be big here," I whispered to Frankie. "Wherever *here* is."

Between the two old ladies sat an even more ancient old guy with white hair and a long frizzy beard that spread halfway out to his shoulders.

All three old folks stared at us.

"Hey, people," I said, trying to be upbeat. "I'm Devin. This is my friend Frankie. From Palmdale Middle?"

While the three old people just stared, the young man turned to us, inhaled a huge breath, and began to speak.

"My name is Jonathan Harker; I am a lawyer from London, England, and I'm traveling here in Europe on business. I am taking this coach into the mountains to meet with a nobleman who lives in a castle in

Transylvania. He has just bought a large house in London and I'm bringing the ownership papers here for him to sign. Then I'm returning to London, where I am engaged to a wonderful woman named Mina. She will be my wife as soon as I return. I'm anxious to return because I've never been away from her or from England and this country seems quite strange to me. The people sitting across from us do not speak our language very well and are highly superstitious about something or other."

I blinked. "Uh-huh . . ."

Frankie looked up from the big fat chubby book and grabbed my arm. "Dev! Everything he said is right here. In the book! It's like he just gave us a summary of what happened so far in the story! Is that cool or what?"

"Cool . . . and handy!" I said. "Hey, wait. Frankie, are you actually, you know . . . reading?"

She gasped quietly, her eyes going big. "I guess so."

"Better you than me!" I said with a laugh. Then I turned back to Harker. "Thanks for all that useful info, sir. Including that bit about the setting. But why don't you keep going with the story so we can get back to school before period two ends and Mrs. Figglehopper gets all mad."

His face made a confused look. "What story?"

"The one in this book," I said, tapping Frankie's book. "We were supposed to be fixing the book, but then Frankie grabbed it, then I grabbed it, and then Frankie did this twisty thing with her fingers, then the zapper gates went all *kkkk!* and there was a crack in the wall and we went into it and then there's suddenly this road and the carriage with the door swinging open and we climbed in and here we are!"

"Wicked summary!" said Frankie, slapping me five.

"What . . . ish . . . book . . . called?" said one woman, eyeing the book as if it were something to be afraid of.

"*Dracula*, of course," Frankie said, smiling. "It's—"

"Akkkk!" the old people shrieked. "Akkk! AKKKK!"

They pulled away as if we had just burped garlic or something. Then they pointed their bony fingers at us and muttered words over and over in a weird language.

"Is it something I said?" Frankie asked.

Jonathan Harker turned to us. "They are talking among themselves about the legends in these parts of Transylvania. Legends of evil spirits and creatures that prey on poor travelers. Why, the innkeeper at my last stop even put a holy medal around my neck, 'to ward off the evil that lurks,' she said. But I am a lawyer. I come from London. It's 1897—nearly the twentieth century!—and I'm afraid legends seem rather silly to me. I don't believe a word of them."

"Not legends!" said one of the old women. "It is all true! At midnight tonight, the evil things in the world will come out. The dark castle you are going to is the very center of evil! Count Dracula is evil!"

"Bad evil!" said the other woman. "*Very* bad evil!"

"Dracula isss a . . . *vampire!*" the old guy hissed.

Harker forced a laugh. "What! Dracula, a vampire?"

"That's somebody who drinks blood," said Frankie. "Believe me, we did an awesome report on the guy."

"But that's just silly!" Harker insisted. "Count Dracula is a very educated man. I am delivering legal documents to him. I have the documents right here."

He tapped his travel bag.

"Except that I think the old folks are right," Frankie said, flipping ahead in the book a few pages. "Dracula *is* a vampire. The book probably even says so. Let me see if I can find a place. Okay, here. It's actually written as if it's your diary. You're in your room at his castle and you're shaving and you cut yourself and . . . yeah! Listen to this! 'When the Count saw my face, his eyes blazed with fury, and he suddenly made a grab at my throat—' Wait a second. The words are getting all blurry. I can't read it. Hey—"

28

Suddenly the carriage began shaking wildly from side to side. The air crackled with electricity. Frankie and I were thrown hard to the floor. Everyone started screaming. The horses reared and took off like rockets.

It felt like the whole scene was cracking open right in front of us. A jagged rip opened in the air above us and got wider and deeper. Soon it would be over us.

Frankie clutched my arm. "Help!" she cried.

"Double help!" I yelled.

But our cries were drowned by the horrible sound of the ripping air and the wild screams of the driver—

"We're going to crash!"

Chapter 6

I slammed the book shut.

Suddenly, everything was normal again. We were all back in our seats, riding along as if nothing happened.

Harker was still tapping his travel bag and saying, ". . . I have the documents right here."

My eyes bugged out. So did Frankie's.

"Time out!" I cried. "Emergency huddle!"

Frankie and I huddled.

"Awesome instant replay!" she whispered.

"Holy crow!" I gasped. "You know what?"

"Our book report shouldn't have been so lame?"

"No," I said. "Well, yeah. But no, what I mean is, I figured something out. Somehow that book of yours is *controlling* what happens! And the people around us—"

"You mean the characters?"

"Whoa! Yes! The characters! Good one. Anyway, they can't learn something before they're supposed to find out in the book. I think maybe we're not allowed to just jump ahead in the story."

"No page jumping, huh?"

"No," I said. "Something bad happens. You said the words get all blurry. And the next thing you know, the whole world starts to crack apart and get all brutal."

Frankie made a face. "That was fairly ugly. So, it's like, if you flip ahead, it ruins the story or something. But are you saying that the only way out of this story is to read every word all the way to the end of the book?"

I nodded sadly. "I think so. Forgetting for a second that all of this is fairly impossible."

"The most impossible thing ever!" she said. "So if we can't go home yet—which, by the way, is going to make us way late for lunch—I guess we'd better do some serious reading."

"Which sounds so bad, I think you'd better start."

"Thanks a lot," Frankie snarled under her breath. "Something tells me this book isn't the biggest barrel of laughs in the world."

"Then we'll just have to add our own laughs," I said. "Otherwise it'll take forever and be fairly deadly."

"Death is all around us!" the old man blurted out.

I glared at the guy. "Way to lighten the mood, dude."

As we traveled steadily up into the mountains, Frankie opened the book. Right away her forehead wrinkled and she began moving her lips silently.

Soon snow began to fall. It whirled around us in thick swirls. The road ascended steeply into the mountains, but still the driver whipped his horses to go faster.

Then we heard strange howling coming from all around us. It sounded as if every animal in the neighborhood was wailing at the same time.

"What's that?" I asked. "The Twilight Bark?"

"Wolves!" the driver called down as if it was an everyday thing. "They are hungry for . . . people."

Frankie turned to me, wrinkling her nose. "It's going to be a full-time job making it through this story."

Suddenly Harker bounced up in his seat.

"I see it!" he said. "The castle!"

The coach slowed, then turned up a narrow curvy road. Soon we entered the walled courtyard of an enormous ancient castle.

"Dracula's lair of evil!" the driver yelled down.

"Everybody out who wants to visit vampires!" one of the old ladies said, giving Harker a queer look.

Then the old mustache guy stared at Frankie and me. "You two and your book, leave us now!"

"Have a happy," I said as they kicked the carriage door open. "Not!"

The courtyard was gloomy and large and black. We stepped out onto rough black stones in front of a giant black door that was old and studded with huge black nails. Above it, tall black windows glared down at us like blind black eyes.

"Check it out, everything is black," said Frankie.

"I'm with you," I said. "Mr. Wexler probably has a word for the way they use colors in a book."

Frankie nodded. "I bet the color thing is a clue. Like now. When everything is colored black, it probably means like nighttime and darkness and fear and scariness and terror and stuff."

"That's pretty much how I feel right now," I said.

Frankie grinned. "See, it works!"

Just then, the driver dumped Harker's luggage off the top of the carriage and drove away from the castle as if he were on fire.

"Well, he gets no tip," said Frankie.

"Strange traveling companions, aren't they?" said Harker. "Still, I can't wait to meet this Dracula fellow!"

I gave him a look, but he just smiled and adjusted his curly hair and his tie and knocked politely on the big scary wooden door. "Oh, Count Dracula! Harker, here!"

Tap, tap, tap. No answer.

The snow was coming down pretty heavily now, so we all huddled close on the doorstep.

Harker whistled a bit, then tapped again. "Count?"

No answer still.

"Hey, castle!" Frankie yelled, pounding on the door. "Open up! Period two is gonna end soon!"

Finally, we heard steps approaching the door from the inside. Then there came the sound of rattling chains and thick burglar bolts being thrown aside. After that, a key turned in the lock with a loud scraping noise. Then another bolt was thrown aside.

"Open it, already!" I said. "We're freezing out here!"

Errrch! The huge door cracked open.

But as cold as we were, it was nothing to the chill we felt when we saw who had opened the big wooden door.

Chapter 7

Standing in the doorway was a tall old man.

Right away, we knew it was him, the dude himself.

Count Dracula, King of the Vampires.

Also known as Mr. Fangy, Old Prongteeth, Dr. Puncture, Professor Neckman, and Old Man Thirsty.

He had sharp, pale features and eyes that glistened strangely in the snowy light.

His nose and chin were long and pointy. His hair was a weird combination of black and white and slicked back, but with three or four crooked parts in it.

He was dressed from head to foot in total black, including a long cape that billowed out behind him.

"He's way into the black thing," Frankie whispered.

"Until something darker comes along," I added.

"I am Count Dracula," the man said, his voice all echoey and distant as if he was talking in a garbage can.

I wished he were in a garbage can.

"I was not expecting . . . three . . . of you," Dracula said, glaring at Frankie and me. As we entered, we spotted for the first time that his eyes had a reddish glow to them. His lips were very red, too.

Frankie nudged me. "His lips match his eyes. Very stylish. Unless . . . oh, wait. Red eyes are not good."

Also not good were the very sharp, very white teeth he showed as we stepped in.

"He must use a tooth whitener," I whispered.

"And a sharpener," Frankie added.

Dracula took us through the entrance area to a large room. The first thing we saw was a fireplace as big as a garage. A fire was crackling in it, but it gave out no heat.

The room was ice cold.

"This must be the living tomb," said Frankie. "Sorry, I mean living room."

It was decorated like a tomb, too. The wall hangings were all torn. There were massive cobwebs drooping down from the ceiling. And there were hundreds of dust bunnies collecting in all the corners.

Dracula bowed to Harker. "Please follow me."

He grabbed an unlit torch from the wall, lit it in

the fireplace, and went up a huge winding staircase. At the top, he hung a left into a long dusty passage. After that passage was another, then another, and another. After three sets of stairs and four dark and winding passages, Dracula finally threw open three heavy doors.

"In these rooms," he said, "you—and your friends—will be comfortable."

"Splendid!" said Harker, as if everything were all normal. "Wonderful house, by the way! The woman I'm engaged to, Mina, would love what you've done with it."

Harker seemed totally clueless.

When Dracula smiled and bowed to Harker, I saw him giving me and Frankie a look that said he was anything but clueless. He was bad, he was evil, and I think he knew we knew it, even if Harker didn't.

I needed to see if that was true.

"Cozy rooms," I said. "Except for the smell of . . . mmm . . . vampires?"

Dracula's eyes flashed, but he said nothing. Then he opened a fourth door. Inside was a big table with a huge meal spread out on it. He stepped in and waved his hands over the table. "Food, after your long journey."

Then, looking right at me, he said, "Have a . . . bite!"

I nearly choked. "Did you say . . . bite?"

Dracula stepped toward me. "Did you say . . . neck?"

I backed away. "I'm pretty sure I didn't. . . ."

Dracula turned to Harker. "Please eat. I will read the documents you have brought from London."

"Certainly, my good Count!" Harker said, smiling broadly. He handed Dracula a thick envelope, then sat down at the table and dug into his meal.

Right. As if chomping on chicken is what you do with a vampire hovering next to you.

Dracula grinned a sly grin, showing those sharp teeth again. He slit open the envelope with a fingertip.

That's when I noticed that his fingernails were cut in long, sharp points—uckkk! Plus, there was hair growing in the middle of his palms—double uckkk!

When he finished reading the papers, Dracula smiled. "The documents seem in order, Mr. Harker. Ah, I can't wait to see England and live in my new house!"

"Carfax Abbey," Harker said in his explaining voice. "It is big and old and a bit run-down, I'm afraid."

"Not that Dracula would notice," said Frankie.

"I am glad that Carfax is old," Dracula replied. "I love the dark shadows of ancient places. I love the night and creatures of the night. The howling wolf. The flying bat. I love when the wind breathes coldly through the broken battlements—"

"That's my favorite, too," said Frankie.

"Ah, yes?" said Dracula. "Good. But now, if you'll excuse me . . ." He stepped over to the door.

"It was a great pleasure meeting you," said Harker.

"Thank you," said Dracula. "I must go now."

"That's an even greater pleasure," said Frankie.

Dracula growled under his breath, then stepped out into the hall, closing the door behind him.

"I can't believe it," I said when I was sure he was gone. "It's actually him!"

Frankie nodded. "He's not just a movie monster. It's really him. The real Dracula. King of the vampires. Right here with us."

"King of vampires, oh, tut, tut," said Harker, leaning back in his chair and patting his stomach. "Our rooms are well lighted and warm, the roast chicken was tasty, and there are at least three kinds of cheese on this table! Vampire? Pish-posh! Dracula is very polite and educated. It may be a strange land, but it's never too soon to say thank you for such hospitality—"

Suddenly, the door sprang open and Dracula leaned in. "I nearly forgot to say, you may go anywhere you wish in my castle, except where the doors are locked. If you wander there, you may find danger. You may find darkness. You may find unspeakable terror. In short, you take your life in your own hands! Sleep well!"

Dracula flashed a toothy grin at us, then closed the door sharply and was gone.

"Hospitality, huh?" I looked at Frankie. "Is it too soon to say . . . *gulp*?"

Chapter 8

Harker rose from the table, tossed down his napkin, and stroked his chin. "I admit Dracula is a bit quirky—"

"Quirky?" I said. "How could you not pick up those clues? The guy's a vampire! Like the old dude in the carriage said: Those big sharp teeth are made for biting!"

Frankie agreed. "The hair alone ought to tell you the guy is not normal. He has four crooked parts going on!"

"And those fingernails!" I said. "And did you see the hairy palms on the guy? It's like—uck!"

Harker was nodding through this, then said, "But you must remember, we are travelers here. A man such as the Count is bound to seem unusual. It doesn't mean he's terrible. . . ."

"Cha!" said Frankie. "He's worse than terrible! And don't go calling him a man. First of all, I found out he's hundreds of years old. Second, he's fairly undead. Believe me, I've been reading and I think we need to leave this castle right now. If we stay, we may not be as alive as we are now."

I nodded. "Translation: This guy is definitely going to put the bite on us. On our necks. With teeth!"

Harker smiled at us. "Don't be so concerned. Speaking of necks, I'm going to my room. I need a shave. It's been a long journey and I must clean up."

I looked at the guy. He wasn't getting it. Not at all.

"Shave. Right. Good. Uh-huh. But with a deadly vampire lurking, you really should be thinking about staying alive, not looking all neat."

"But I'm all stubbly," Harker said, running his fingers up and down his chin. "It's good I brought my own shaving mirror. I don't see one around here anywhere."

"Because vampires don't like mirrors!" Frankie said.

"Would you, if you looked like Dracula?" I asked.

She nodded. "It so explains the hair."

Harker just kept stroking his chin. "Yes . . . yes . . . a nice close shave." Then he went to his room and closed the door quietly, whistling a merry tune.

I blinked at Frankie. "The guy is clueless. A clue, he does not have. Of clues, he is out."

"No clues anywhere near the guy."

We mulled it over. "It's the book," I said finally. "Harker can't know what's going on before it goes on."

"And I guess we can't tell him," said Frankie. "It'll all be blah-blah-mumble-mumble to him. It doesn't matter what we say."

"Which is good for making jokes about Dracula," I said, "but bad if we want people to believe us. So, what do we do now?"

"Well, I'm not sure of all the rules," said Frankie, "but I was peeking in the book just now and I found out that there are rooms in the castle where we haven't been yet. I figure if the author writes about them, somebody must see them. That means we should be able to go exploring. Maybe we can find a way out of the castle."

I grinned at my friend. "That sounds pretty excellent."

Carefully, I opened the door Dracula had closed on us and peered out to the hall. The gloom before us was lit by a couple of faintly flickering candles mounted near the ceiling halfway down the hall. Beyond the candles were the stairs leading down to the next level.

"Could it be any scarier?" I muttered.

Frankie grabbed a candle and held it close. "Let me see what the book says."

"'Gulp,' probably," I replied.

Together, we made our way to the stairs and climbed down step by creaking step. To make matters worse, the wolves had begun to howl outside again. I shivered.

"Frankie, did you get to the fun part of the book yet?"

"Harker is shaving," she said.

I snickered. "Right. But I was thinking of the fun part where we go home and play sock ball—"

"That's not what I mean," she said, trembling as she read the book. "You remember that page I read in the coach? Harker was shaving and . . . and . . ."

I gasped. "And Dracula attacked him!"

Frankie pushed the book at me. "It's right here. I'm too scared to read it. You read it. Hurry!"

Being careful not to rip the pages that we had fixed, I took the book and found the part Frankie had read to Harker earlier in the carriage.

"Got it," I said. "Harker's shaving and he cuts himself. 'At that instant . . . I saw that the cut . . . had bled a little . . . and the blood was trickling over my chin. When the Count saw my face . . . his eyes blazed with fury . . . and he suddenly made a grab at my throat.'"

I stopped reading. "Frankie—his throat!"

"That's right where his neck is!"

"Vampires bite necks!"

"And it's happening now!"

"Hurry!"

We charged back up the staircase in a mad scramble to reach Harker's room before anything bad happened. We ran as fast as we could. Maybe a little too fast.

The moment I took the final corner at full blast was exactly the same moment that Frankie decided to give her sprint one final burst of speed.

Wham! I crashed into her and fell forward.

The first thing I felt was the top of my head go slightly flat. It's like those slow-motion replays of a bat hitting a baseball, and though you would never believe it, the bat actually flattens the ball a little bit when they connect.

Imagine my head as the ball and the door as the bat.

Wham! Crunch! Luckily the door couldn't hold against the force of my speeding head.

It burst open with a bang. The door, I mean.

When we sailed into the room, it was all happening just as the book said. Dracula's eyes were redder than ever and his lips were super plump. And he was lunging at Harker. But the worst part was that his white hair was darker than before. His cheeks were puffy and full. And there were drops of blood on his long, pointy chin. He looked half as old as when we first saw him.

"He's been feeding!" Frankie exclaimed. "It talks about that in the book. He attacks poor innocent people and lives off them! And he's getting younger!"

Harker had a very surprised look on his face, a blot of blood on his chin, and he was staggering backward to the window, saying, "Oh, my! My, my! Oh!"

Ignoring us, Dracula lurched at Harker, his eyes swollen like big red golf balls. His mouth was wide open and his sharp huge teeth were sticking out like a mouthful of new chalk all ready to bite.

"I am hungry!" Dracula said, licking his lips.

"But, Count," said Harker, "I don't understand. . . ."

Frankie jumped to Harker. "Look at the mirror! It shows you and me and Devin—but no Dracula. See— Dracula *is* a vampire! That's proof!"

Dracula exploded in anger. He pushed Frankie to the floor, then made a grab at me. His grip was icy cold and as strong as an animal's. With a single move, he launched me at the wall. Then he turned to Harker again.

Suddenly, a flash of silver came from Harker's throat. It was the holy medal the innkeeper had given him. Once Dracula saw it, he pulled back instantly, shielding his face from the glinting medal.

"Ahhhh!" he howled. At once, he flung open the heavy window and hurled himself through it. We rushed to the casement and popped our heads out. The drop was straight down a hundred feet to the courtyard.

But there was Dracula, clinging like a lizard to the wall below the window.

"You shall not leave my castle!" he hissed at us. "You are—all of you—my prisoners!"

Then, with a snarling laugh, Dracula began to crawl down the side of the castle, *facedown*, his cloak spreading out around him like a pair of giant wings.

Chapter 9

It was horrible to watch.

Dracula's fingers actually dug into the spaces between the stones as he edged slowly down the castle wall.

Harker drew back into the room, set his jaw firmly, and shook his head. "This is the creature I am helping to get to London?"

"I'm afraid so," I said. "Now do you believe us?"

"We must escape," said Harker, trying the door, but finding it suddenly locked. "There must be a way. There are doors, doors, doors, everywhere!"

"And all locked and bolted," Frankie said, holding up the book. "It says so here. We are prisoners!"

"There's got to be a way!" I said.

Frankie kept reading. "Wait a second. There is a way. But you're not going to like it. I think we have to . . . follow him."

"Follow him?" I said, blinking at the open window. "You mean . . . follow him . . . out the window?"

Frankie nodded, pushing the book right under my nose and pointing to a sentence. I read it. It was about climbing out onto a narrow ledge. I stepped to the window and peeked out to the awesome depths below.

"Oh, man!" I groaned. "We're dead for sure!"

"It seems to be the only way," said Frankie, her eyes still glued to the page.

I thought and thought and looked and looked and finally I realized she was right. There was no other way.

"Okay," I said. "I mean, it's only a book, right?"

Frankie gave me a look that said she wasn't so sure.

One after another, all three of us climbed out the window and onto a narrow ledge of stone that ran around the castle. The stones were big and cut roughly, so it wasn't too hard getting a grip on them. Slowly—*very* slowly—we edged out across the outer wall.

"Dracula's room is . . . below . . . down there," said Harker, huffing and puffing and nearly losing his grip. "Let's hope . . . he hasn't locked . . . his own . . . room."

"Good thought," I said.

It took us about two hours of slow climbing, but we finally made it to the casement of another window. His eyes crazed with fear, Harker yanked at it until it opened. We slid feet first through the window into a dark space. Harker was right. It was Dracula's room.

There were spare capes everywhere and lots of dust.

"Uck!" said Frankie, gagging on the thick air. "I love that we're not clinging to the side of a castle wall a hundred feet above the ground, but seriously, how can that vampire live with all this dust?"

"I think the clue is that he doesn't live with it," I said. "He's undead, remember?"

"Thanks for the reminder," she grumbled.

Harker spotted a heavy black door beside the ash-filled fireplace. "Let's try this," he said. Together we pulled it open and found a dark set of stairs circling down steeply into what I guessed was the castle cellar.

We listened closely for a while and heard nothing. Harker nodded to us. Taking the lead, he tiptoed down the stairs, and as we followed him, our noses were attacked by a heavy, thick odor.

"It smells like a sewer," I said, pinching my nose.

"We do visit all the best places," Frankie said.

At the bottom of the stairs was an old, ruined cellar. Pale yellow moonlight streaked in through a cracked window and allowed us to look around.

"This must be a sort of chapel," said Harker.

The cellar's ceiling was low and partially caved in. Tumbled stones lay everywhere, amid mounds of dirt piled across the floor. But the strangest thing was the boxes. Dozens and dozens of long wooden boxes.

They looked like coffins, only the lids were off of some of them and we saw that they weren't filled with bodies. They were filled with dirt.

"Whoever heard of putting dirt in a box?" I asked.

"Flower boxes have dirt in them," said Harker.

I laughed. "Somehow I don't think Dracula is into gardening."

Being good with numbers, Frankie did a quick count of the boxes. "Fifty boxes," she said, dusting her hands.

"But why are they here?" asked Harker. "What are they for? It's all so strange and mysterious—"

"I'll find out," said Frankie. She plopped down on a box that stood in a patch of yellow moonlight, cracked open the book, and stuck her nose deep into it.

"Wow, Frankie," I said. "First you count, then you read? Someone here's going to get a major headache."

"Probably," she admitted. "But it makes me not so scared if I know what's going on."

"I can dig it." And I could. It's like watching a scary movie a second time. You know what's going to happen and you aren't as scared as you were the first time.

While Frankie was straining her eyesight, and Harker poked around the chapel for a way out, I found something interesting. On the side of each dirt box was a label, and all of them said the same thing.

From Dracula's Castle
To Whitby, England
Handle with Care

For some reason, it made me mad that the evil vampire was asking people to handle him with care.

"Ha!" I snorted. "I'll handle with no care! None! You big vampire creep face—"

Next to me was a box with its lid on. I gave it a hard kick and the lid just happened to slide aside.

What I saw made my heart stop.

He was inside the box. Yes, him! The Count, in the box. He was lying on a bed of dirt. His eyes were closed, but his face was even plumper than before. Blood trickled from the corners of his mouth. And he was smiling.

"G-G-G-Grosssss!" I finally managed to say. Harker ran over and, seeing who was napping in the box, grabbed a nearby shovel and whacked Dracula on the head. It didn't seem to hurt him at all. He hardly budged an inch. In fact, all that happened was that the vampire's face turned to us, and his eyes popped open.

"Yahhh!" I cried. I kicked the lid back over his face, and we jumped back, expecting Drac to bounce out. But he didn't. I guess he was just so tired after his snacking that he didn't want to get up.

Scared and shivering, Harker and I edged back to Frankie, who was reading so deeply she hadn't heard us yelling and batting vampires with shovels. I was about to tell her what we'd seen when I realized something.

We were suddenly not alone.

It's not as if there were a noise. I didn't actually hear anything. It was more of a feeling running up my neck.

At least I hoped it was a feeling running up my neck and not fingers running up my neck. I turned slowly.

Standing there, in the yellow moonlight, were three women. At least they had been women . . . *once.* Now they were three thin, pale, probably dead, ex-women.

My heart nearly stopped beating.

The women stood in the shadows staring at us. They wore long, dirty gowns. Their skin was color-less, but their eyes were bright and hard, their teeth white, and their lips red and gleaming.

They might have passed for supermodels on a photoshoot in a castle, except that they cast no shadows on the floor, they smelled really bad, those nice white teeth were actually fangs, and like their vampire boss, their eyes were flashing red.

"Um . . . Harker?" I said.

But Harker was even more scared than I was. He stood there, silent, staring, and frozen to the spot as the three vampires took a single step toward us.

"F . . . F . . . Frankie?" I mumbled.

"Shhh," she said, her back to us, her nose deep in the book, not seeing anything of what was going on. "In case you haven't noticed, I'm reading here. Plus, I found the part where we're in this basement."

"Frankie, I have to tell you something. . . ."

"Shhh," she repeated. "Harker's telling how he finds the dirt and the boxes. And there's the yellow moonlight. It's all here on page fifty-four. This is so cool!"

"Skim ahead, will you? I need to know what hap-pens on, say, page fifty-five."

"Skimming isn't reading!" she said sharply, still

glued to the page. "Mr. Wexler told us to read every word. Besides, there are lots of strange words in this book. . . ."

"There are also lots of strange people here and I think they want us dead!"

"You really know how to break somebody's concentration, Devin," Frankie said with a sigh, shutting her book and turning to Harker and me. "Now what strange people are you talking about—"

The three women stood staring at Frankie, their fangs glistening in the moonlight.

Frankie paused a moment, then said, "Oh."

Then she said, "OH!"

"Now do you see what I mean?" I said. "Strange people. Strange ladies. Although I'm pretty sure the technical term is lady vampires. Three lady vampires. One for each of us. And I figure if we don't want to get to know them a lot better, we need to get out of here."

Frankie nodded slowly. "You just read my mind."

"Oh, great! I learn to read just before—I die!"

At that moment, the three vampires ground their sharp teeth together and—with a very creepy, wet, rushing sound—they attacked us.

Chapter 10

Luckily, my legs turned to jelly, and I crumpled to the floor. The first lady vampire couldn't stop in time, and she fell over me and into a box.

"Get them!" she howled to the others, spitting dirt from her mouth. "They belong to us!"

Well, that was pretty much the creepiest thing I'd ever heard! But there was no time to think about it.

"I'll take the dumb one!" the second vampire said.

"Which dumb one?" the third asked.

"Hey!" said Frankie. "Now it's personal!"

As I wobbled to my feet, Frankie hurled a shovel at the charging vamps.

Wump-wump-wump!

They crashed into a wall and let out a wild hissing

sound that made my skin crawl. In the second that they were all down, Frankie grabbed me and Harker, and all three of us tore straight up the stairs we had come down.

My heart was racing like a motor. My head was pounding like a drum. We kept running and didn't stop to catch our breath until we were back in Dracula's room. We rushed in and bolted the door behind us.

"Close shave," said Frankie.

"Close shave!" I cried. "We nearly died! We've got to get out of this book—"

Suddenly we heard the sound of cracking whips and the pounding and scraping of horses' hooves from outside.

"What new evil is happening now?" said Harker.

We jumped over to the window and flung it open in time to see five large wagons roll into the black-stoned courtyard below.

The lead driver shouted in a strange language to the others, and the wagons slowed to a stop. Men hopped out and entered the castle far below. A moment later, they began loading the big long boxes into the wagons.

"Those are Gypsies," said Harker. "What sort of game is Dracula playing here?"

"My guess is he's taking his boxes to England," I

replied. "They were all filled with dirt, labeled, and ready to go."

"Right," added Frankie. "It's not like he can just bop around whenever and wherever he wants. Vamps have to work the night shift."

Harker's eyes were wild. "But . . . but . . . if they are taking Dracula's boxes to England, he will go with them. And that means . . . we will be left here prisoners in this castle . . . with them. With those horrible—"

Blam! Blam!

The vampire ladies began pounding on the door, wailing loudly, "We want you! And we'll get you!"

"Oh!" Harker suddenly blurted out. "We are trapped! Trapped like rats! Could any dream be more terrible than this horrible gloom and mystery that closes around me! Oh, dear! Dear, dear!"

I guessed he was talking lines from the book, but I had to admit it did look fairly grim for us. I turned to my friend. "Frankie, there's only one thing to do," I said. "We need to end this chapter. End it right now."

"What? You're not thinking of . . ."

"Exactly. Jump ahead in the book. We need to get out of here. If we flip ahead a couple of pages things could be better. I mean, how much worse could they get?"

Womp! Womp! The vamps were hurtling themselves against the door now.

Frankie looked scared. "But what about the big ripping sound and the darkness coming at us and everything going nutty-nutty?"

Poing! One of the hinges popped off the door and flew across the room. The door sagged toward us.

"One for each of us!" the lady vampires wailed.

"Flip the pages, Frankie!" I cried. "Get us out of here!"

Harker's eyes grew huge. His skin was as white as a pillowcase. "We're going to die! Die, die, die! Oh, good-bye, everyone! Mina, my love, I shall try to escape home to you. Until then—good-bye! Good-bye!"

"Frankie!" I cried. "Flip the pages! Flip them—now!"

She gave me one last look, then flipped the pages.

The room cracked from top to bottom with an enormous ripping sound. Darkness poured out of the rip, and we were all thrown to the floor.

The walls, the ceiling, the furniture around us . . . everything went black and swirly.

Everything in my head went black and swirly, too.

Then—*kawooooom!*—there was nothing.

Chapter 11

The next thing I remember was that I was on my back and water was splashing my face. Correction, I was on my back, then my front, then my back. I was rolling.

"Help!" I screamed.

Suddenly a hand grabbed me. I hoped that the hand wasn't all hairy with its fingernails cut to sharp points.

It wasn't. The fingernails were painted pearly white.

"Frankie!" I cried.

"One and the same!" Frankie dragged me to my feet.

I wiped the water from my eyes. "Where are we?"

"On some kind of ship," she said, struggling to keep her balance. "And there's a major storm going on."

It seemed true. We were on a flat wooden deck crammed with wet stuff. Waves were sloshing up really high, then crashing down again.

"The ship is called the *Demeter*," Frankie went on, bending over the book to keep the old pages dry. "It says so right here. Actually, it's not Harker's diary anymore. It's a clipping from a newspaper."

Icy rain pelted us like heavy fists. To make it worse, thick fog poured over everything and choked the air.

"I don't want to be on a ship," I said, trying to keep from falling overboard. "I don't like ships. They roll from side to side, and pretty soon my lunch starts thinking about reappearing."

"You won't like this ship for another reason," said Frankie. "It's full of boxes—"

"Boxes!" I shrieked at the top of my lungs. "Boxes! Boxes from Dracula's castle? Boxes of dirt?"

"The baddest, evilest dirt ever," said Frankie, pointing to the deck behind me where the long wooden coffins were tied down with thick ropes.

I staggered, then clung to Frankie for support. "So, like, how many pages did you actually flip?"

Using her finger and thumb to mark the places, Frankie said, "About thirty pages."

"No wonder we blew a fuse!"

"At least I don't see Pastyface Neckbiter around anywhere," Frankie mumbled. "Those spooky vampire sisters, either. Which, let me tell you, is good news. The bad news is that when we changed the setting, I think we left our old pal Jonathan Harker behind—"

There was a sudden crashing jolt, and we were thrown to the deck. Staggering to our feet, we noticed that the boat didn't rock back and forth anymore.

"We must have run aground," said Frankie. "That means we've landed!"

"The best part of being on a boat," I said.

We scrambled to the railing and, looking over, found that the storm had driven the ship up onto a beach. There were cliffs surrounding us on all sides, with a small town nestled between them and a harbor below.

"Cute little town, no castles in sight, I like it!" I said.

Grrrr. Something growled.

I turned to Frankie. "Did you just growl at me? Please say 'yes.'"

"No."

Grrrr!

We whirled around to see a big black dog spring onto deck from inside the ship. It clacked its jaws at us and bared its enormous teeth as if it were going to charge, but a giant wave washed over Frankie and me and sent us sliding across the deck. That wave saved us.

Growling once more, the dog leaped twenty feet off the deck to the harbor below and hightailed it across the sand.

"Not that I want to follow that creepy thing," I said, "but we should probably get off the ship, too."

"Aye-aye, Captain Dev!"

We spotted a big gray hulk of a building standing in the fog nearby. When a blast of wind came up over the water I could see that the building was a church. It looked fairly safe.

We climbed off the ship and ran across the beach, taking cover from the storm under the peaked front roof of the church. While Frankie read the book to see what she could find out, I took a look around.

In the flashes of lightning, I saw that the church stood nearby a small graveyard of old, tilted stones. They made me shiver, as just about everything had since we had dropped into this book. The shivers convinced me that, even though the setting had changed, we were definitely in the same story.

"I found it," said Frankie, pointing to the page. "The storm, the church. There should be a woman—"

"You there! You!" a woman's voice shouted.

"Right on schedule," I said.

We turned to see a woman running toward the church. She was dressed in a long cloak, but her head was bare, and her long brown hair was tossed by the wind. She looked very scared about something. Probably about being in a horror book.

"My goodness!" she cried, rushing under the roof to us. "Are you all right? What are you doing here?"

Frankie and I glanced at each other. We knew the truth wouldn't help much. "We're new in town," I said. "By the way, what town is this?"

"Why, it's Whitby, of course—"

"Of course, of course!" Frankie whispered. "The labels on the dirt boxes were addressed to Whitby. So, we're in England now."

"Cool," I said. "Lady, we're Frankie and Devin."

"My name is Mina," she said. "Mina Murray. But soon my name will change to Mina Harker."

Frankie jumped. "Hey, we know you! Your boyfriend Jonathan told us about you—"

Mina nearly hit the church roof. "My goodness! Jonathan is in Europe even now! How do you know him?"

"We just left him in Dracula's castle," I said.

"Which is pretty much a lair of evil," said Frankie.

"Dracula was the man Jonathan was going to see!" Mina said. "Please—tell me everything you know."

"Why, sure," I said. Then I took a deep breath.

"It all started with me turning to chat with Frankie in Mr. Wexler's English class this morning. . . ."

Ten minutes later I finished with, "So I told Frankie to flip the pages. And she flipped the pages! Everything went all *kkkk!* and here we are."

When I finally stopped, Mina was staring at me as if I were some kind of idiot. It's a look I am familiar with.

"But what does that mean?" she asked.

"Which part?" I asked. "I said a lot of stuff."

"Everything you said was nothing more than a confused mumble of noises!"

I was stunned. She hadn't gotten a word of my long and detailed summary. I was bummed. All that effort!

Then Frankie pulled me aside.

"Devin," she whispered. "I think we just discovered another wrinkle to this book thing. Even though all the Harker stuff at the castle happened before, Mina doesn't know it happened before. The author must be playing around with his characters. The reader knows what happened at Dracula's castle, but some characters don't."

I tried to take it all in. "Does this mean we have to convince everybody all over again?"

Frankie chewed her lip. "Maybe we'd better just

push the story along." She turned to Mina. "So, what brings you out on such a dark and stormy night?"

"I came looking for a dear friend of mine," Mina said. "Her name is Lucy Westenra. We've known each other for years."

Frankie shot me a quick grin. Yeah. Lifelong friends. We knew a little something about that. "Go on," I said.

"Lucy was staying with me but she disappeared from my house tonight."

There was fear in Mina's eyes when she said this. She was obviously really into her character. She made me believe she really cared for this Lucy person.

"So, Lucy is sort of special, huh?" asked Frankie.

"She is a wonderful friend to me," Mina said, her eyes getting moist. "Everyone loves her. In fact, before she became engaged, three gentlemen had asked for her hand in marriage—"

"Three!" I said. "Wow, this Lucy character must be some kind of babe—"

Whack! Frankie smacked the back of my head lightly with the book. "One more crack like that, Devin, and I'm flipping back to the boat!"

I made a face and rubbed my head. "So . . ." I asked, "where do you think Lucy has gone?"

The wind tore at Mina's hair as she scanned the scenery. "She has been sleepwalking recently so I thought she was doing it again. I heard a sound in the night, and sat up in bed, only to find Lucy's bed empty. I ran downstairs. She was not in the house—"

Kkkk! The sky lit up with a jagged flash of light.

"Oh, my!" Mina shouted. "Look there! It's her!"

The storm was hurling strong wind through the harbor and blowing the fog to shreds. We could just see a figure in white sitting on a bench in the nearby graveyard.

"It *is* Lucy," cried Mina again. "Oh, I have a horrible sense of fear upon me. Let us hurry to her!"

The moment we started for her, a dark shadow surged up behind Lucy's bench. It seemed to grow larger with every leap we took.

Frankie gasped. "Is that the dog? The black dog from the ship?"

"Except it's not a 'dog' anymore," I said, making air quotes with my fingers as I ran. "It's . . . changing. . . ."

In seconds the dog seemed to grow into the shape of a man. In one swift move, it bent over Lucy.

"Oh, my gosh," I said. "It's . . . it's . . ."

"What is it?" cried Mina, running as fast as she could in her old costume.

"Well, it ain't Scooby-Doo!" Frankie snapped. "Hey, you, Bitey Boy! Get away from her!"

The dark thing raised its head. Its pasty white face and red gleaming eyes told us it could only be the terrible fiend himself—Count Dracula.

I saw a flash of black cape in the fog and then a whooshing sound as he rushed away into the shadows of the graveyard. When we got to her, Lucy was alone.

She was young, like Mina, and pretty, so I could understand why so many guys wanted to marry her. But right now she was as white as paper and just about as thin. She clung to the bench as if she were half dead.

"Lucy, my dear, what happened?" said Mina, kneeling next to her. "Who was that person?"

Lucy coughed slightly as Mina pulled a shawl around her and fastened it with a pin at her throat.

"No one was here," said Lucy.

But even with the shawl pulled tight, I saw two small puncture holes on Lucy's throat.

I shot a glance at Frankie. We both nodded. We knew.

"No one was here, huh?" I said. "Then how do you explain those two red marks on your neck?"

"They're pimples?" said Lucy.

"I scratched her when I pinned the shawl?" said Mina.

"I tried to put on lipstick but I missed?"

"She fell on a fork?"

Frankie gave me a look. "Dude, here we go again!"

Chapter 12

With the storm easing up, we all scooted off to Mina's house where she said her friend Dr. Sewer was visiting.

"Dr. Sewer?" I blinked. "They need doctors for that?"

"Not *sewer*, you dummy," Frankie said, pointing to page one hundred and three in the book. "*Seward*, with a *D*. He's one of Lucy's three men friends. But she didn't pick him to marry her."

"I think I need a scorecard," I mumbled.

"What you need," said Frankie, "is to do some reading. It's not impossible, you know. In fact, here. Take the book. My brain is tired. You read for a while."

"Harsh," I grumbled, but I took the chubby book from her anyway as we entered Mina's house. It was a nice place: small, but with cute fluffy gardens all around it.

"Dr. Seward is here at the request of Arthur Holmwood, Lucy's *fiancé*," Mina said as we helped Lucy in.

"Ah, so *Holmwood*'s the one she chose," I said.

When we barged in the front door, a man rushed to help us. He was dressed in a plain dark suit.

"Dr. Seward," said Mina. "Lucy was sleepwalking again. We found her in the cemetery."

"Ah, poor Lucy," said the doctor. We all helped her upstairs to her room. Then Frankie and I stayed in the hall as Mina and Dr. Seward got Lucy set up in bed.

A few minutes later, they came back out.

"She is resting now," Mina said to us. "Thank you."

Dr. Seward shook our hands. "Both of you, thanks for helping. When Lucy's fiancé Arthur asked me to check on her, I didn't dream she could be in such a state."

"State?" I said. "England is a country, right?"

Seward gave me a look, then turned to Mina and smiled. "My dear, the most wonderful letter has come."

Her eyes lit up. "Not . . ."

"Yes! Jonathan is alive and safe," Dr. Seward said.

"All right!" I said. "He made it past the vamp babes."

Mina jumped for joy. "My Jonathan! Where is he?"

"In Budapest, in Europe," said the doctor. "He is in a hospital. But don't worry, we are assured he is all right. He fled Transylvania and arrived in Budapest just days ago. I've arranged for you to take the next boat to him."

"I will meet him right away!" she said, running to her room to pack.

While she was gone, Dr. Seward wrote out a telegram. When Mina appeared carrying a suitcase, he handed the telegram to her. "Please send this when you get to town," he said. "And *bon voyage!*"

"Oh, to see Jonathan again!" Mina cried happily. She raced out of the house and sped toward town singing.

I wondered if we would meet her character again, and I found myself sort of wanting to read ahead, but Dr. Seward called us both into Lucy's room.

She was asleep, breathing quietly. Seward bent over her, holding a candle near her throat. He examined the two puncture holes closely.

"She is so pale and thin," he said. "Her pulse is weak. She seems to have lost a fair amount of blood. And what do you make of those strange marks on her throat?"

"Those strange *puncture* marks?" I said. "Well, it's so obvious. They came from—"

71

"Devin!" said Frankie, making big eyes at me and pointing to the book in my hand.

I understood. "Ah, yes, the clueless approach."

I looked at the ceiling. I stroked my chin and muttered for a while. Then I paced a little. Finally, I said, "Well, doctor, what do *you* make of the marks on her throat?"

"I have no idea. What do you make of them?"

"Well, what do you make of them?"

"What do you make of them?"

"What do you make of them?"

Seward threw up his hands. "This is going nowhere! Luckily, that telegram I asked Mina to send was to my old friend and teacher, Professor Abraham Van Helsing. Van Helsing is a great scientist from Amsterdam who knows more about strange diseases than anyone else I know. Perhaps he can tell us what is happening to Lucy. I only hope he arrives soon, before she gets worse."

He sat down next to Lucy's bed and waited.

We all waited.

Tick-tock, went the clock. We sat for a while. We sat a little more. I stared around. Frankie stared around. Then we both stared around.

"Maybe you should read," Frankie whispered to me. "You know, to push things along."

I grumbled, but opened the book. I looked at

some words. Then I read a sentence. I got to the end of it and read the next one. Then the next one.

The problem was, we had to wait for Dr. Seward's telegram to go all the way from Whitby, England, to Amsterdam, Holland. That could take days. Luckily, authors can make time pass as quickly as they want. About a page later, it happened. I looked up from the book.

"It's talking about a doorbell—"

Ding-dong! The doorbell rang.

I blinked. "Wow, reading works!"

Dr. Seward jumped up and we followed him downstairs. "That will be my old friend Professor Van Helsing now—"

Blam! The door flew open. In barged a chubby little man with large eyes, big bushy hair flying in every direction, a frizzy beard, a long mustache, and a cane.

"Hello, Professor Van Helsing!" said Dr. Seward. "I'm so glad you could come!"

"Ya, is good you are glad!" the chubby man snapped.

"Yes, well, Professor," said Dr. Seward. "We have a patient here. Lucy is her name. She has a strange ailment. She seems to have lost a lot of blood. She is weak and pale. She was seen with a mysterious dark figure. And she has two small puncture marks on her neck."

I was waiting for Van Helsing to start with the clueless chin-stroking business, and the whole what-do-you-make-of-the-marks thing, but he surprised me.

"Ach!" he blurted out in his heavy Dutch accent. "Lucy has attacked by a vampire been! It so clear is. We decide what first to do, yes? Yes! First—flowers I put in her room some."

The guy was really into mangling the language, but he seemed to know his stuff. As if by magic, he managed to pull a huge wad of flowers from his coat.

"Cool!" I said. "She'll like those—"

"They are not for liking!" Van Helsing exploded in my face. "They are for not *dying*!"

Without another word, Van Helsing clomped up the stairs and burst into Lucy's room.

She was propped up in bed, pillows stacked behind her. Her face was even paler and grayer than before. Her lips were thin. Her eyes drooped. Her hair was a mess. She looked even worse than the first time we'd seen her, which was pretty bad. Sorry to say, she didn't look much like a babe anymore.

"I am afraid," said Lucy, clutching at her throat.

"Flowers are for fearing not," Van Helsing said, crunching his words again. "There is much goodness to you in these so common flowers. See, I place in your room myself them. I make a wreath to wear you."

He twisted a ring of flowers into a short garland then placed it around her neck. "Ya, is good."

Lucy coughed lightly. "Professor, the smell—"

"Hush!" Van Helsing said. "We all obey my things."

Next the professor closed the windows and latched them shut. Taking more flowers from his coat, he rubbed them all over the window sashes, then the doors, and around the fireplace.

"This is quite puzzling," Dr. Seward said.

"Your head is a puzzle!" snorted Van Helsing, his mustache flapping as a puff of air shot from his nostrils. "You must believe my flowers! Take care that you not disturb nothing to nothing. Open the windows not."

The professor twirled on his heels and clomped back to the hall, motioning us to follow. "Lucy—rest!"

When her door was closed, Van Helsing said, "I must to back my hotel go now. Things are there needful for the Lucy." Then he paused, looked to both sides, and leaned close. Tapping a finger on the side of his nose he said, "You must all on your watchness put."

I didn't get what he meant. "Excuse me?"

"Do not let your sight pass from her."

"What?"

"The Lucy is dangerous to be unlooked at."

"Huh?"

"Things not Lucy should be blind of you!"

"Say that again?"

"Keep in your eyeballs—her!"

"Huh?"

"Be Lucy the only sight of your vision!"

We all stood staring at him and his floppy mustache.

Finally Frankie jumped. "Are you saying we should watch Lucy, keep an eye on her, and don't let her out of our sight?"

"Ya! What I said!"

With that, Van Helsing thumped across the floor, down the stairs, and straight out of the house.

"Upgiddy!" we heard him yell, and his horse took off.

Dr. Seward frowned. "Now we wait to see what tonight shall bring."

With those dark words, I stuck my finger in the book and rubbed my tired eyes. The chapter had ended.

Chapter 13

The dark and stormy evening turned into a stormy dark night.

Lightning kept flashing outside the windows. Thunder boomed like armies clashing in the attic. And the smell from those flowers was making everyone sick.

Still, we set up outside Lucy's room and kept up the watch. Also the reading. After resting my eyes, I started again. I must have read about twenty pages altogether, some kind of record for me.

When my brain grew sleepy, Frankie picked up where I left off, reading in the flickering candlelight which, let me tell you, is not the greatest light to read by.

In those pages we found out that Lucy's mother, Mrs. Westenra, was freaking out about her and was expected to arrive any time. Also, Dr. Seward was writing about Lucy to some of the other characters: Arthur Holmwood, the guy Lucy was engaged to, and Arthur's American buddy, a dude named Quincey Morris, the third and final person who had wanted to marry her.

Besides getting a whole bunch of new names to keep track of, it wasn't the best part of the book, either, since it was all about how Lucy felt good, then bad, then good, then bad.

Finally we both started to yawn.

Of course, yawn. It had been a really long time since we had hopped on Harker's carriage in period two. I had no idea what time it was. Or even whether it was the same *day* we had left the library.

For some reason, it almost didn't matter. We were in this story now. What was going on back home— wherever that was—didn't seem as important or probably as interesting as what was happening right here and now in Whitby.

Besides, I was fairly sure we would find the zapper gates when we needed to get home. It would probably be at the end of the story that we would find them.

I hoped we would find them. We had better find them!

Just then I heard a strange rumbling sound and shot straight up in my chair. "Frankie, did you hear that?"

She opened one eye. "It was coming from the direction of your stomach."

I looked down. The rumbling happened again. "It *is* coming from the direction of my stomach. And judging by how thick the rest of the book still is, I'm guessing there's a lot yet to happen. So I'll need my strength to get through it. I'm going munchie hunting."

"If you find food, blow a trumpet," she said.

"In the meantime, be Lucy your only eyeballs!"

While Frankie took a quick peek at Lucy, I tiptoed around the house searching for something to nosh. To my surprise I found another whole character downstairs.

She was in the kitchen at the back, a nice, plump lady in a long dress, hat, and coat. She was pacing back and forth, muttering to herself. Thinking she was waiting for someone to bring her into the action, I decided to help her get some lines to say.

"Hey, lady, I'm Devin," I said, giving her a little wave. "What's your name?"

"I am Mrs. Westenra, Lucy's mother," she said.

"Wow, her mom. Yeah, we read about you," I said.

"I've just arrived. It was so quiet, I didn't want to

disturb my Lucy, but how is she feeling, the poor dear?"

I felt bad. Her mom had to know the truth, but it was really hard to say. "Lucy's . . . um . . . so-so."

"So-so what?"

"So-so not so good. But on the plus side, Professor Abraham Van Helsing's on the case. He's got this really big accent so he sounds very smart."

She seemed to take some comfort from that and sat down at the table. "I wish I could help her," she said. "Perhaps I'll make her something to eat—"

Rrrr. It was like my stomach actually heard that word.

"Um . . . did you say *eat*? As in eat *food*?"

"Why, young sir—you're hungry!" she said, springing up and tying on an apron covered in a whole menu of food stains. "Oh, I can whip up something for you, poor darling. What would you like?"

I happily named all my favorites, but she had never heard of peanut butter, corn chips, waffles, pizza, or cheese in a can, so I went for something simple. "Spaghetti?"

Mrs. Westenra beamed. "I know that one! Now, all I have to do is find some pasta, tomatoes, cheese, onions, peppers, garlic . . ."

Already my mouth started to water.

I went back to Frankie to tell her about Lucy's

mom and the coming feast when we heard a bunch of noise from outside. Taking one last look to see that Lucy was okay, we hurried downstairs to look. We crept past Dr. Seward who was asleep in a chair and went out the front door to the path.

Peering through the storm at the harbor below, we saw several long wagons and a group of men unloading something from the abandoned ship. With all the scraping and dragging, they were making quite a racket.

We watched for a while before we saw what they were unloading. When we did see, we were stunned.

"The boxes!" I gasped. "I almost forgot about them. They're taking the boxes away! Ooh, that's probably not so good. Where are they taking them?"

Frankie opened the book. "The words are too fuzzy to read. But I bet we'll find out before too long. And I bet wherever they go, we'll be following. I smell another change of setting coming up."

"And I smell tomato sauce!" I said, turning back to the house. "Let's go stuff ourselves until we're sick!"

"Or just before!" Frankie added.

The feast was delicious. Frankie and I gobbled two whole platters of the stringy stuff, then asked Mrs. Westenra for seconds, thirds, and fourths.

"Book food is good," I said as I slurped down the last strand of spaghetti. "I feel not so empty now."

"It's the garlic that makes the difference," the cook said. "It spices up the sauce something wonderful. No need to have Lucy's room so stuffy with all that garlic!"

"Garlic?" said Frankie. She opened the book. "But—"

Suddenly—*wham!*—the front door burst open.

"Patient is how?" boomed a voice. A moment later, Van Helsing stormed into the kitchen to find us up to our ears in spaghetti sauce.

"Patient Lucy!" he repeated. "How is?"

Mrs. Westenra made a little bow. "Well, if she's better, I'm the one who's done it!"

"What do you mean?" asked Dr. Seward, coming into the kitchen rubbing his eyes. "I say, what's going on?"

Lucy's mother smiled. "I was looking for some ingredients for sauce for the young master—"

I raised my hand. "That would be me."

"Well, and don't you know my nose told me there was something pungent in my Lucy's room!" the lady went on. "So I went in there and my! I found just what I was looking for. Garlic. Lots of it. Oh, but it spices the sauce something wonderful!"

Van Helsing's face turned as gray as his raincoat. He began to shake and shudder and sputter and spit.

"But . . . achhh!" the man exploded. "It was garlic

on the Lucy to protect her from vampires! Now! Now! To the Lucy—let us hurry!"

Van Helsing led the charge on Lucy's room. He battered open the door with his fists only to find Lucy's window shattered and a huge black bat with red eyes fluttering out.

"Ach! My strudel! No!" Van Helsing cried.

There on the bed lay poor Lucy. She was more white and pale than ever. Even her lips were white, and her gums seemed to have shrunk back from her teeth, which were longer and sharper than before.

"The fiend has been here and Lucy's blood is gone!" Van Helsing shouted. "We need blood to go in her, not out!"

"Hurry!" cried Dr. Seward. "Hurry, or Lucy will die!"

Stunned at how things were suddenly going, I opened the book and read as fast as I could for the next hour.

With Van Helsing helping, Dr. Seward gave Lucy a blood transfusion. That's where you take blood from a healthy person and give it to a sick person. It worked for a while, but then Lucy got weak again. I kept reading and found out that the next night there was a big black bird at her window. The night after that there was a wolf trying to break in.

On the third night, Lucy got out of the house

somehow while everyone was dozing. Nobody knew where she went, and Lucy herself didn't remember anything.

That's when Arthur Holmwood and Quincey Morris finally entered the scene. Holmwood, Lucy's fiancé, was this very English guy with perfect manners and a fancy velvet vest. But Morris was a big blustery American and tramped around like a cowboy in a tight suit. I guess he was the author's idea of a Texan from Texas. He was all "howdy" and "gosh" and "man alive!"

Frankie and I liked him right away.

Both Holmwood and Morris gave Lucy blood transfusions, too, but nothing seemed to work.

This went on for over a week.

Finally, one morning, Van Helsing, Dr. Seward, and Holmwood did their usual check on Lucy while Frankie and I stayed in the hall. When they came out, Holmwood was crying, and Van Helsing's face was all sad and droopy. He shook his head. "No . . . no . . . no . . ."

Frankie looked at me. Her eyes were wet.

It was a fairly unfunny and grim moment.

We walked down the hall together. Finally, Frankie stopped. She pointed to the book in my hands.

"Lucy . . . um . . . sort of . . . dies . . . doesn't she?"

I skimmed the next couple of pages until the

words got a little blurry. Finally, I had to nod my head.

"I'm pretty sure she does, Frankie. Sorry."

"Oh, man. We've made some wrong mistakes before, but the garlic mistake is one of the wrongest."

"It was sort of in the book anyway," I said. "Lucy's mom really does take the garlic away. But, yeah, I guess we all goofed up pretty major."

Frankie was way bummed. I hated to see her like that. I became bummed, too. I could imagine that we might just want to give up on the whole book. The story was just too sad in a lot of ways. But then I realized that the story had to keep going. It had to, or we'd never get to the end.

"On the plus side," I said, trying to lighten the mood, "she's only a character in a book."

"But you get attached, you know?"

"I noticed that. But on the plus-plus side, Lucy doesn't really die. She becomes one of the undead. Dracula recruits her to be a vampire and she starts doing the biting thing on other people. Think of it as a career move. Not a good one, but a move."

She almost smiled. "Thanks for trying to make me feel good, but I gotta ask. Why do people write sad stories?"

I shrugged. "Why do people read them?"

"That was heavy, Devin. Very heavy."

"It must be all that spaghetti I ate."

She snorted a laugh at that. "Dude, I know what you mean. Mine isn't sitting too well, either."

Over the next half hour, Frankie and I took turns reading the sad pages about Lucy's death. She died, was buried, then became a true vampire, attacking and biting people living in Whitby. Van Helsing convinced everyone that they had to perform a ceremony on Lucy by driving a wooden stake through her heart. He said it was the only way to cure a vampire.

It was brutal. But we found we couldn't stop reading until we were standing outside Lucy's tomb. By then, all the guys had done the ceremony to stop Lucy vamping around the neighborhood at night. It was pretty sad and gross, but at least it was over.

Van Helsing stared at Frankie, Dr. Seward, Holmwood, Morris, and me, the wind swirling his frizzy hair.

"It is done," he said. "Lucy is no longer of the undead. She is now just plain dead."

Dr. Seward shoved his hand in his pocket and pulled out a letter. "Today, I received news from Jonathan Harker and Mina. They have returned from the hospital in Budapest and are now in London. And they have seen Dracula there—"

"Then go to London we must!" Van Helsing announced. "Two nights from now, we will all meet at the home of Dr. Seward in London to plot our next move."

I nudged Frankie. "A sort of big meeting of the guys."

"There's always one of those when you need to get a job done," she said. "I love the big meeting of the guys."

"Me, too," I said. "Big meetings of guys always make you feel good. Let's do it."

Everyone looked at each other and nodded.

By the next page, we were in London.

Chapter 14

Dr. Seward's house in London was stuck between a hospital on one side and a dark old house on the other. Although it was rainy and cold and the fog was thick, it was still warm and cozy inside. A fire crackled noisily in the fireplace as we gathered around the dining room table.

While Van Helsing paced up and down, Morris chewed a big cigar, and Holmwood sat frowning in a corner. Not only was Lucy dead, but Holmwood's father had just died, so now everybody was calling him Lord Godalming. Sort of a mouthful, if you ask me. I turned to Frankie and checked her place in the book.

We had a lot of pages left.

"Shouldn't we start the big meeting of the guys?" I asked.

Van Helsing shook his head. "We are waiting for—"

"More characters?" said Frankie. "I mean . . . people?"

I looked at her. She looked at me. People. Right. They did seem a lot more real now than when we had started.

"We wait for the doorbell," said Van Helsing.

I gave Frankie the old head nod, and she began reading. Suddenly, she jumped up and rushed to the door.

Ding—!

Frankie pulled the door open before it *dong*ed, and Harker and his wife Mina stumbled into the room.

"Mr. Harker Jonathan and his wife of charms, Mina!" Van Helsing boomed, clasping their hands. "I am with so much pleasure meeting you now both!"

Then with a snap of his fingers, the professor bid us all to sit down and start the meeting.

"Begin us now!" he said. "First, Harker Jonathan, what say you?"

Harker stood up and glanced at all of us one by one. He looked tired and scared. "Dracula is in London," he said. "And though it seems impossible, he appears to be younger, stronger, and more powerful than before. Not only that, but with Mina helping me, we have tracked down the boxes of dirt—"

"Evil dirt!" I said.

"Bad evil!" Frankie added.

"Ya—quiet!" said Van Helsing. "And the dirty boxes are where?"

"They were unloaded from the boat at Whitby and brought to the house Dracula purchased," said Mina. "An old house in London known as Carfax Abbey—"

"Oh—my—gosh!" Dr. Seward exclaimed suddenly, jumping up from the table. "Carfax? Carfax? Carfax!"

"Carfax Abbey," said Frankie, pointing to the page.

"But—Carfax Abbey is—the house next door!"

Dr. Seward pointed out the window at the dark hulky shape beyond the trees. It looked ultraspooky.

"Astounding it is!" said Van Helsing. "Right here?"

I gasped. "That's some kind of coincidence!"

"All fifty boxes were brought to the chapel at Carfax," Harker went on. "I've been asking, and it seems Dracula has purchased three other London houses, but I know not where. Some boxes may have been moved around."

"We must destroy all the boxes," said Lord Godalming—formerly Holmwood—from his chair. "To avenge my dear, dear Lucy!"

"What I want to know," drawled Quincey Morris, his cigar held tight between his teeth, "is why there is silly dirt in the boxes. Man alive! Back in America, we leave dirt on the ground—where it belongs!"

"Ah!" said Van Helsing, puffing up his chest. "I will turn on your brain with lightedness! Now you listen!"

It was clear that Van Helsing had been waiting for this moment since he first stepped into this book. He stuck his hands in his pockets and began to stomp back and forth in front of us dramatically.

"Vampires!" he began. "What can we say of them?"

"They have fangs," I said.

"They dress in total black," said Frankie.

"They live in dusty castles," said Harker.

"And more much!" said the professor, raising his finger. "Vampires have been wherever people are. In old Greece, Rome, Germany, France, India, and China—"

"How about the U.S.?" Frankie whispered to me.

"Also there!" Van Helsing said.

"Yeah?" Quincey snorted. "Over my dead body!"

"Now listen of my words," the professor resumed. "The vampire dies without dying. He grows younger when he has fed on the lives of the living. Ya, also, he throws no shadow on the ground. He make in the mirror no reflect of himself. He can be wolf or dog or bat or bird. Being undead he only become stronger and stronger, with more power to work his evil wickedness on the world. Dracula is now as strong as twenty men. He can command the dead. Also the rat, the owl, the bat, the moth, the flea, the spider, and the wolf. He can become them and also grow or become small. He at times vanish himself and become unknown!"

"So, he's pretty much invincible?" I asked.

"Ah, no!" the professor went on. "He can do all these things, but he is free not. He may not enter where his invitation is not. His power stops at break of day. If sunlight is on him, it does not tan him. It burns him up! A wooden stake piercing his heart will kill him, *poof!* And Dracula needs a coffin of evil dirt from his foul castle to sleep every night!"

"That explains why his coat is always so dirty, but why does he need fifty boxes of the stuff?" I asked. "Why not just one?"

Van Helsing let out a little smile from under his puffy mustache. "Ah, can we not all guess why Dracula needs fifty such dirt boxes?"

I raised my hand. "Because even though he's a Count he can't count?"

Van Helsing shook his head.

"Because he's evil, bad-evil?"

He nodded. "Ya! But no!"

"Ooh!" said Frankie. "For when he takes road trips?"

"Maybe ya, but no. . . ."

I gasped. "Because he's building an army! An army of vampires! And the dirt is for their slumber parties!"

"YA!" Van Helsing exploded, stomping his foot joyfully. "You have hit the nail on its hat!"

"But how will we trap him?" Godalming asked.

The professor twirled on his heels. "We destroy him with the stake of wood! *Pfft!* In his heart. *Kapushhh*, he turn to dust!"

"Count me in, Professor," said Morris. "I'm itchin' for a fight with this varmint."

"I am with you, too, Professor," said Godalming. "For Lucy's sake. This Dracula grows more evil every hour."

"More than much!" Van Helsing exploded. "That is why the vampire must be destroyed! But first, we find his where!"

"His what?" Harker asked.

"Not his what—his where! We must find where is his where!"

"Where is his what?" said Harker.

"What will he wear?" said Morris.

Suddenly, there was a crashing sound and the window shattered into bits. A dark furry shape dove into the room, flapping thick black wings.

"A bat!" said Dr. Seward. "Could it be—?"

Mina, who had been fairly quiet so far, screamed. "Out! Out! You terrible ugly thing!" She rushed to the bat and struck at it wildly. She pulled her hand away quickly and the bat flew back out the window and away across the lawn to Carfax next door.

Harker rushed to his wife. "Mina, you are bleeding."

"I'm fine," she replied. "Barely a scratch."

Van Helsing frowned. "But it could have been—"

"It was just a bat, Professor!" Mina said sharply. "It wasn't Dracula. I'm sure of it! I feel perfect. Perfect—do you hear! Now, you men go on to Carfax alone. I'll be fine here. More than fine, in fact. I'll be perfect!"

"Is good!" Van Helsing said. "Now, let us go to the Carfax hurringly. Water I have, that is blessed and holy. Ya, everything Dracula is not. We sprinkle and *sss!* we sterilize his filthy dirt boxes of filth. That way, Dracula has a place to sleep nowhere. Ya! We must find this vampire and drive him out!"

"Drive?" said Frankie. "Let's make him walk like everyone else!"

As we all stood up, it suddenly seemed like one of those special moments of bonding. Without a word, we clasped our hands together. Frankie had to put the book down on the table to do that. It was the first time, I think, that either of us had done that. But I think it meant something.

It meant that we were part of the story now.

I turned to Frankie. She seemed to feel it, too.

"This is the 'let's go' part of the book, isn't it, Dev?" Frankie asked.

"I think so," I said. "There's only one thing to do and everybody knows it. Go ahead, Frankie. Do the honors."

Taking a deep breath and looking around at all the
everybody . . . let's go!"

elsi g sputtered under his thick
e go! I the vampire expert

ne was looking at him.
go!"

we went, Mina chirped hap-
perfect, you know!"

Why does she keep saying

he doesn't have too many

Chapter 15

As we made our way across Dr. Seward's lawn, Carfax Abbey stood against the darkening London sky like a huge stone ruin.

"They must have used one giant pile of stones for this place," I murmured to Frankie.

She snorted. "Now the stones want to be a pile again."

It was true. The place was totally falling down.

The gates in front were of old wood and even older iron all eaten with rust. It took no more than a minute to push through them and enter the big over-grown yard.

The house loomed ahead. There were only a few windows in it, all of them dark. Iron bars crisscrossed the glass—which should have told us something.

"Lair of evil, number two," Frankie mumbled as we climbed up the front steps.

At the door, Van Helsing raised his hand. "My friends, we are going into terrible danger. Be watchful!"

At the professor's signal, Harker and Seward pressed on the door. The rusty hinges creaked. Slowly the old door opened.

I had been prepared for some kind of smell, but the stench that came blowing out nearly knocked us over.

"Oh!" Harker said, burying his nose in his coat.

"Ach!" Van Helsing exclaimed. "Every breath of that monster Dracula clings to here! But we must proceed."

I sniffed my armpits as we entered.

"Let's find the boxes quickly," said Godalming.

Harker, for some reason looking right at me and Frankie, said, "Why don't you two come with me. We've done this before, haven't we?"

"And it was such fun the first time," I mumbled.

Van Helsing nodded sharply. "You find boxes. We other men will examinate every cranny and nookle to discover some clue about the where of Dracula now."

As Harker headed into the dark interior of the vampire's evil lair, I nudged Frankie. "You afraid?"

"Nah!" she said. "Well, maybe a little. Okay, I can't move. But Dracula's not here, right? And it's only boxes, right? With no dead folks in them? Just dirt, right?"

"Probably," said Harker, not very reassuringly as he pulled us both with him. "Now let's hurry. Mina is alone. I want to get back to her as soon as possible."

The other guys wandered off into the darkness, leaving Harker, Frankie, and me to follow the damp smell of evil dirt all the way into the Carfax chapel.

The chapel, when we got there, was crammed with dust. The floor was inches deep with the stuff. If you can picture it, the walls were actually fluffy with dust! Masses of spiderwebs in the corners were so thick that they looked like old rags hanging in midair.

It was dusty and dark, but you couldn't miss all the big wooden boxes lined up across the floor. We all got to work counting them. Even me.

Harker finished first. "I count twenty-nine boxes."

"That's what I get," said Frankie. "Devin? You?"

I held up all ten fingers. "Six more boxes than this."

"Sixteen?" said Frankie. "How did you get sixteen?"

"Or maybe it was eight," I said, looking at my hands.

"Eight?" said Harker, frowning. "Eight what?"

"It was eight," I said. "No, wait. Five. It was ten boxes plus five. Well, minus the one finger I used to point and count. So four plus ten."

Frankie grumbled. "You're saying there are fourteen boxes here?"

"Except that I needed a finger to scratch, so you can't count that. But then I used my kneecaps to count back up again."

"So . . . thirteen plus two. Fifteen? Fifteen boxes?"

"But then I remember scratching one kneecap."

Frankie's eyes blazed. "Devin!"

"Plus I picked my nose, so you can't count that. But then both nostrils added another two—"

"DEVIN!"

I looked at her. She was mad. My fingers were all twisted up and one was in my nose. "Twenty-nine boxes sounds just about right," I said.

When we told the others, Van Helsing announced that we needed to find Dracula's other houses immediately to locate the other twenty-one boxes. It was like he was the boss or something. But we did what he said. It was because of his accent, I think. He was just so good at it.

So when Van Helsing, Seward, and Quincey Morris left Carfax and went to east London, Godalming, Harker, Frankie, and I went to central London. We traipsed around the foggy old city in the middle of the night waking people up and asking if they saw boxes of dirt. Some of them actually had. Lord Godalming even did his "I am a powerful and fancy person" speech to a bunch of folks and got them to help us.

It was nearly dawn when we all met outside Carfax Abbey once more.

As we headed back to Seward's house, the professor tugged on his mustache and asked, "Well, and how smart are we now?"

"Six boxes each were shipped to two houses in East London," said Morris.

"Is twelve!" said Van Helsing. "And the remaining nine?"

"Delivered to a black ruin of a house in central London in Piccadilly," said Harker.

Frankie laughed when she heard the word. "Piccadilly. That's such a funny name—"

"Is not funny!" snarled Van Helsing, stomping his foot. "If I am right, this Pillydilly house is the key to Dracula. It is his hindquarters!"

"Headquarters," said Dr. Seward softly. "Headquarters."

"Ya—what I said! And now we must go there—"

Suddenly, a loud bloodcurdling scream tore the air.

Harker froze where he stood. "That sounded like

100

a woman's scream. And from very nearby."

"Holy cow!" said Frankie, nearly jumping out of her skin. "I knew there was something wrong, but I just couldn't put my finger on it."

"Are we talking about nose picking again?" I said.

"No!" said Frankie. "Mina kept saying she felt perfect, right? But she isn't perfect. She's in trouble!"

"What's that you're saying?" said Harker, his eyes ablaze. "Mina? My Mina? In trouble?"

Morris waved his arms around. "But, man alive, the lady said she was perfect!"

"Frankie's right!" I said, finally getting it. "Mina was saying she was perfect way too many times. It was right after the bat came in and we were too wrapped up in the story and the boxes and our own thoughts to notice what was happening. The bat bit her. In fact—"

Another scream sounded.

"Mina!" Harker shot out of there like a rocket.

"Follow now him we must!" Van Helsing said. "His Mina is in harm!"

We ran as fast as we could back across the lawn.

The first thing we noticed at Dr. Seward's house was lots of broken glass on the front walk.

Then we heard Mina scream a third time.

Then came an awful hissing noise from Mina's room!

Chapter 16

When we crashed into Mina's room, what we saw made our hair stand on end and our hearts stand still.

Harker had arrived only seconds earlier but was already lying in a heap on the floor.

Mina knelt near the edge of the bed. By her side stood a tall, thin man, dressed entirely in black. His face was turned from us, but we all knew who it was.

"Dracula!" I shouted. "You creep-head!"

He turned at once. He was lots younger! He looked like a young man. His hair was black. His skin was no longer wrinkled and craggy.

When he saw us, his eyes flamed red and his sharp white teeth dripped red, too.

"Count Dracula, you fiend!" said Seward.

"That's our Mina you're biting!" cried Godalming.

Dracula threw Mina roughly to the floor. "You fools! You idiots in your English suits with all the buttons—you cannot stop me!"

"But try we will!" came a cry from the door. Van Helsing finally burst in after huffing up the stairs. He advanced toward the vampire with a wooden stake.

"Ha!" Dracula laughed. "You are too late. I have shared my blood with your precious Mina. She will be my companion, my helper, my bride—"

"Eeeww!" said Frankie.

"She will help me defeat you," Dracula said. "When I call her, she will come. I can speak to her mind across the miles. We are . . . the same. But enough talk—"

Instantly he sprang at us. At the same time, Van Helsing whipped something out of his pocket and held it up.

Dracula screeched to a stop, hissing loudly. Van Helsing was holding a silver holy medal in his hand.

"Back, you dark creature!" the professor intoned.

Further and further back the vampire cowered, shielding his face as he had done back at his own castle.

Suddenly, the moonlight failed, and a big black cloud sailed across the sky, plunging the room into darkness. Everybody yelled. Frankie and I jumped for Dracula, but thudded on the bare floor instead. When finally Quincey Morris lit a match, we saw that Dracula had vanished, leaving nothing behind but a wisp of bad-smelling fog escaping under the door.

A moment later, a large bat shrieked and squealed from outside as it flapped across the yard and high over the trees into the paling night.

"It is *him*!" Van Helsing shouted.

As he did, Mina let out a scream so wild and ear-piercing that if the window hadn't been broken already, it would have shattered right then. We all rushed to her.

Her face was as pale as a sheet, and the only color on her was red from the drops of blood on her neck. Her eyes were consumed with terror. "He bit me," she said. "I felt my strength fading away. Then he spoke. . . ."

"What said him?" asked the professor.

"He told me that I would be special. He said that our minds are joined together. When he called me, no matter where he was, I would find him and join him. I would help him in his terrible work!"

Harker shook his head. "And we let the horrible creature escape!"

"Ah," said Van Helsing, tapping his forehead. "But I think I know where he goes. To his final where!"

"And just where is his where?" Godalming asked.

"Pillydilly, that's who!" replied the professor, stomping his foot. "We go. We stop the fiend. We do it now!"

Leaving Mina resting calmly and safely at Dr. Seward's house, and after Van Helsing had sterilized the boxes at Carfax with holy water, we raced to Piccadilly in a horse-drawn carriage. We piled out before another of those haunted-houselike places Dracula seemed to go for.

"Gosh, that's some lair of evil!" muttered Morris.

"We keep finding them," said Frankie.

The lair looked as if no one had been living in it for a long time. Which in Dracula's case was true. The windows were encrusted with dust and the shutters were closed, except where they were falling away from the walls.

We entered the black house and within minutes found a bunch of keys to Drac's other dirt-box houses. Godalming and Morris took off to destroy the boxes there, while Dr. Seward, Harker, the professor, Frankie, and I set out to find and destroy the nine boxes remaining in this house.

We found eight boxes.

"Eight!" Van Helsing exploded, stomping both feet, pulling his hair, twisting his mustache nearly off, and clacking his teeth together. "Shtink! Shtank! Shtunk!"

"Excuse me?" said Frankie.

"Our work is not done! He has hid a box! One box!"

For the next hour, we turned the broken-down old house upside down—which wasn't hard to do—searching for Dracula's final box.

Nope. It wasn't there.

Frankie looked worried. "Devin, I'm getting—"

"Scared?" I said. "Yeah, me, too."

A little while later Morris and Godalming returned, happy that they had destroyed the other twelve boxes, but sad when we told them about the box that got away.

After that we waited for *him* to return.

"There is danger for us," the professor said. "We need many arms of many kinds."

"I've got two," I said. "The regular human kind."

"I think the professor means weapons," said Morris.

"Ya, weapons!" Van Helsing said. He tapped a black bag that he'd brought with him. "Wooden stakes, to kill the vampire . . . if we need them."

We didn't have to wait long. As we shivered in the cold house, we could hear the sound of footsteps clacking up the walk.

"Get ready for the Drac attack," I said.

Blam! With a single bound, a dark shape burst

through the door and leaped into the room. There was something so like a panther in how he moved. When the Count saw us, a horrible sort of snarl passed over his face. Then he showed his fangs as we all jumped at him.

Harker was in the lead. "You wretched beast!" he cried. "I shall pummel you."

He launched himself at the vampire, but it was Harker who was pummeled. Dracula tossed him back like a puppet and Harker crashed into the wall and crumpled to the floor, mumbling in a daze.

The Count turned on Dr. Seward next, pushing him roughly into Godalming and Morris. All three tumbled out the door.

Van Helsing charged forward quickly, holding his foot-long wooden stake out firmly. As he lunged at the vampire, however, Dracula hurled a chair, hitting the professor in the leg and sending him flopping onto a table. With a single, swift bound, Dracula leaped for Frankie and me, growling and hissing.

Luckily for us, Morris and Seward bounced back to their feet and charged at him.

Dracula swept his arms up and knocked both men back.

"Ach, he is strong!" Van Helsing said, unflopping himself from the table. "But we are stronger! Take a stake and a holy medal!"

Dracula howled like a wolf as we advanced on him, stakes in one hand and holy medals in the other. His skin turned a greenish-yellow in contrast to his burning eyes. His whole face showed hatred and rage.

Then in a sort of animal leap, he dived over us, dashed across the room, and threw himself at the window. Amid the crash and glitter of the falling glass, he tumbled to the flagstones below.

"He loves the window escape method," Frankie muttered. As we ran over we saw him spring unhurt from the ground. He ran across the yard, his cape swishing around him, then turned and spoke to us.

"You think you have stopped me. But you have not!"

Van Helsing grunted and shouted back. "But we shall find your last box of evil dirt! You will have no place to be. At sunrise—*pfft!*—you will burn like a potato!"

"At sunrise?" howled the vampire. "How much more evil can I do by then? My revenge has just begun. I shall live for centuries until the world is ruled by vampires. And I shall be their king! And as for my final box of dirt, you shall never find it. In it, I shall live forever!"

With a hateful snarl, Dracula jumped away across the lawn, vanishing into the night.

"Again!" Harker cried, pounding his fist on the window frame. "Again, he has escaped our grasp! All because of one little box of dirt, Dracula will keep on biting and biting and biting. He will live forever and ever and ever and ever and ever—"

I turned to Frankie. "It sounds pretty bad when he says it like that."

"Devin," she said, her eyes suddenly wet. "It is bad."

Chapter 17

Everybody was bummed out and depressed about Dracula's escape when we met back at Dr. Seward's house later that morning. When Mina saw our faces, her own went as pale as death itself. It finally got to me how bad things really were.

"Listen people," I said, "we can't let Dracula keep on escaping and living forever to bite more people and turn them into a huge army of biting vampires. Somebody around here has got to have a plan!"

Harker sat in the dining room, calming Mina as best he could. But she looked worse and worse. I was scared she was becoming a vampire right before our eyes.

Van Helsing and Dr. Seward paced the room, back

and forth, back and forth. Quincey Morris and Lord Godalming muttered quietly to themselves. Frankie was chewing her lip and frowning, stopping only to sigh and shake her head. It wasn't a jolly group, for sure.

I raised my hand. "Someone *does* have a plan, right?"

"We got nothing!" Van Helsing said. "There is one more earth box. But where it is . . . we know not. Dracula has fled away, and there is no knowing where his goneness has taken him."

They all sighed and shook their heads. It was terrible.

I looked at Frankie. "Dracula is evil," I said.

She blinked. "Well, duh."

"No, I mean, he's evil and he's hurting these people." I looked at them in the fading candlelight.

"Frankie, you were right when you said that you get attached. I didn't really think about it before. But you're right. It's the people in the stories that make people read books over and over."

She nodded finally. "And why books get chewed up and libraries have to get kids like us to fix them?"

"Exactly. And I want to fix this book. I mean really fix it. Give me the book, Frankie."

"You mean you're going to read?"

"We need to stop Dracula," I said. "You've been doing most of the reading. Now it's my turn. The answer's in the book. I'm going to find it before it's too late."

A smile crept over Frankie's face as she handed me the book. "Read, Dev," she said. "Read like you've never read before!"

I cracked open the book and did just that.

I read as fast and as well as I could. I didn't understand some of the words, but I got most of them. And I didn't stop reading until I had the answer. After what seemed like hours, I knew what had to happen.

I stuck my finger in the page and jumped up.

"What is it?" said Frankie.

Without answering, I marched directly into Mina's room. She was sleeping.

"Mina," I said loudly. "It's all up to you."

She opened her eyes and sat up in bed. And then she said exactly what was on the page where my finger was.

"Go call the professor. I want to see him at once!"

In a few seconds everyone was crowded by her bed.

"Ya, what is?" said Van Helsing, rubbing the sleep from his eyes.

"Professor," said Mina, "you have to hypnotize me."

"Of course, of course—*what*?"

"If what the Count said is true," said Mina, "then there is some kind of a connection, a mental link, between me and him. If Dracula can speak to my thoughts, perhaps we can listen to his thoughts through mine. And by listening, we may be able to find him!"

The professor's face lit up. "Ya, is an idea!"

Looking fixedly at Mina, Van Helsing began making passes in front of her face, from over the top of her head downward, with each hand, one after the other. It all looked like mumbo jumbo to me and Frankie, but soon her eyes got droopy. At last, she sat completely still.

"Man alive," said Morris. "It's working!"

"Mina, where are you now?" Van Helsing asked.

Her voice was soft and sleepy. "I am lying still. It feels like . . . death. Yes! I am . . . in my final box of earth!"

"Ach, it is true," the professor said. "Go on, go on. What do you hear?"

"The lapping of water," Mina replied dreamily. "Little waves leap and crash. There is water all around. I can hear it on the outside."

"The outside?" said Harker. "The outside of what?"

"The hull," said Mina.

Van Helsing jumped to his feet. "This is good! Good! We have no moments to lose! Dracula have take his last box of earth on board a ship. But where is he . . . where?"

"Moo," mumbled Mina.

"Moo?" I said.

"*Cows* are mooing!" Mina said. "And I hear wagon wheels not far off, turning, turning. . . ."

Van Helsing crooked his finger at us. "Dracula is going up one of the narrow rivers that lead to his homeland! I know where! He returns to—Transylvania!"

"Transylvania?" said Dr. Seward. "But supposing we track him down and find him—then what?"

"Then we him destroy!" Van Helsing stated. "We must do it. For if he escape us this time, the Count may sleep for a century then come alive—"

"A century?" Frankie gulped. "Devin, when was this book written?"

I looked at the pages in the front of the book. "About a hundred years ago."

"That's almost a century!" she said. "Dracula could come back during our time! We need to stop him now."

"But he's far ahead of us," said Harker, beginning to pace in front of us. "We may not have time to catch up."

"We can catch up," said Frankie. "And there's only one sure way to do it. Devin, we need to flip the pages!"

I gave her a look. "But, Frankie, I don't think—"

"If you won't do it—I will." She grabbed the book. "Hold on to your wigs, everyone, because I'm flipping!"

And she did.

Kkkkk! There was a bright flash, then the room went dark and everyone toppled to the floor screaming.

The air, hot at first, grew icy cold, then hot again, as if it couldn't make up its mind. The darkness we had seen twice before came down again, piercing the room in half like a ripping page. Some of us were on one side, some on the other. I saw Frankie being pulled away from me as the spear of darkness widened and widened.

"Frankie!" I cried out.

"Devin!" she yelled back.

But the darkness overcame everything. I fell hard to the floor. Then the room, the table, and all the furnishings were suddenly gone.

I was lying on the rough ground.

The cold rough black ground.

Mountains loomed all around me. A cold and icy wind whipped down from the frost-covered treetops.

And I saw it, perched on a nearby summit, a dark hulk against the gathering darkness.

"The castle!" I said, nearly choking. "The castle of Count Dracula!"

Chapter 18

A hand grasped mine. It was old, but strong.

"Up with you," said the familiar voice of Professor Van Helsing. He stood with Mina, staring at the castle.

"Where are the others?" I said, gazing around the dark landscape. "Where's Frankie?"

"We had to split up to better track the evil vampire's movements," Mina said. "Frankie is with Lord Godalming and my Jonathan, chasing the fiend by boat."

The professor nodded. "Quincey the Morris and Dr. Seward are by land coming, on horses with many rifles. We three have pushed ahead, with Mina helping, to where Dracula must come, if he fool our friends."

I stared up at the castle, that awful place of everything creepy and grisly. I shivered. It was then I realized that not only was Frankie not there, neither was the book.

I gulped. I hoped Frankie was all right and that she had the book safe and sound. I wasn't looking forward to staying in this story forever.

"So what happens now?" I asked.

"We wait for the Count," said Van Helsing. "I have just come from the castle where the three vampire sisters have found true death from me. Also with the holy water, Dracula's tomb is made too holy for him."

Gazing up at the castle and rubbing her forehead, Mina said, "He is coming. I can feel it."

Mina was pale and thin and worn down by what must have been a long journey. There was a strange look in her eyes and I remembered again what Dracula had said about her. She *would* be one of his vampires, a special one. A glance from Van Helsing told me that he was worried about that, too.

As if on cue, the mountain wolves began to howl.

Then, just like the first time I was here, snow began to fall, sweeping cold white flakes into the darkening air.

"Soon he is come," said the professor. "So let us find a waiting place. When he be come, we be ready!"

As we made our way down from the castle, I felt something wild and frightening about the whole place. Night was falling. Soon it would be dark. Dracula was coming. All the old fears came rushing back. I didn't like it. But what I liked even less was what was right there in front of us.

"Look, look!" cried Mina. "Coming up the road!"

Straight before us and not far off came a group of Gypsies on horses galloping wildly toward the castle. In the middle of the gang was a long wagon.

On the wagon was a great big box.

I nearly swallowed my head when I saw it.

"It's him! Mr. Floss-a-lot! Fangmouth! Dr. Dental!"

"Dracula," said Van Helsing grimly. "King of Vampires!"

"Yeah, him."

As if we were all thinking the same thing, the three of us jumped behind a large rock and crouched there, waiting. The wagon driver lashed his horses violently and they sprang with greater speed toward the castle.

"They come quickly," Van Helsing whispered. "Racing for the sunset. If Dracula rise from his box, and our friends come not soon, we may be too late!"

Closer and closer the Gypsies came, hurtling over the road toward us. The sky was growing darker, streaking us with shadows from the setting sun. Our wooden stakes ready, we watched the wagon lurching closer.

I was so scared, I wanted Frankie to be right there. And I wanted her to have the book. I wanted to read it and read it and read it until this scene was finally over.

"There are too many of them!" I said. "We need help!"

Suddenly, there was a loud crackling sound. Everything seemed to light up and get dark at exactly the same time. We were all thrown up in the air and bounced back down again. Smoke whooshed in from nowhere. We all started coughing.

Then a voice pierced the fog.

"Stop that wagon!"

I knew that voice! It was Frankie!

"Frankie!" I cried. "You're here! You're here!"

And she was—charging out of the smoke with Harker and Godalming by her side. Not far away were Dr. Seward and Quincey Morris galloping at top speed on a pair of raging horses.

"Man alive, we're here just in the nick of time!" Morris shouted. "That old sun's nearly down!"

But the Gypsies drove even more wildly to the castle.

Seeing our friends, Van Helsing, Mina, and I felt bold. We jumped up from behind our rock and stood in the road.

The Gypsies were going to drive straight over us,

but before they knew what was happening Harker and Quincey forced their way to the wagon.

"We must finish this before the sun sets!" Harker shouted. With strength that seemed incredible, he leaped onto the wagon and pulled on the heavy box. In one move, he flung it over the side of the wagon.

"Man alive!" Morris cried. "I mean, vampire alive. I mean undead. I mean . . . get him!"

We formed a wall around the box, but the Gypsies swarmed us, weapons drawn. One of them wounded Morris with a knife, but Godalming and Seward pulled out their rifles and the Gypsies shrank back.

That left only us . . . and *him*.

All this time, Harker was kicking at the box and pounding on it. "Dracula! Dracula! You evil fiend! I'll get you for what you did to my Mina!"

Suddenly—*kkkkrrrrk!*—there was the terrible sound of splintering wood.

As the last rays of sunlight faded below the horizon, the lid of the box burst open and Dracula bounced out, hissing like a leaky balloon.

"Sooooo! You think you can stop the great Dracula? What can a boy, a girl, a woman, and a few weak old men do against the king of vampires? Why are you even here? Don't you see my enormous fangs?"

His mouth shot open and his teeth, as long as a

bunch of bananas, sparkled in the fading light.

"He ask too much question!" Van Helsing said.

But I raised my hand. "The answers are: yes, lots, the book brought us here, and is that broccoli between your fangs? Because if it is, you really need to floss—"

Dracula narrowed his red eyes at me, then glanced at the sun as it finally sank below the horizon.

Sunset. Breakfast time for vampires.

Dracula's look of hate turned to triumph.

And my legs turned to jelly.

Growling like a panther, Dracula swished his cape and opened his mouth as wide as possible. "Prepare to die!" he snarled.

"Think again, Dracu—loser!" yelled Frankie.

Without warning, the Count leaped away from his box of dirt and thrust himself in my direction, leading with his teeth. But he didn't get far.

Harker and Morris leaped on him, their knives drawn. There was a sweep and a flash of silver in the moonlight.

"No! No! I—must—bite—you!" Dracula cried.

"Bite the dust instead, Fangboy!" said Frankie.

Trying to jump out of the way, Dracula slipped on his cape, and Harker and Morris made their final attack.

"Ugh!" groaned the vampire, as their knives pierced his evil heart.

KKK-POOOOOOOOF!

The vampire burst into a million tiny little chunks. They sprayed everywhere in a large cloud of foul-smelling dust. Dark flecks exploded over us, across the road, and into the distant trees.

Finally, there was nothing left. Just flakes of fluffy white snow whirling swiftly through the night air.

"Rest in pieces, Count Dracula," I said. "Your part in this story is over."

"Ya," said the professor. "The undead king is now just plain *dead*!"

Thinking we had something to do with the sudden vanishing of the man in the box, the Gypsy horsemen and the wagon driver finally fled out of there at top speed.

It was peaceful.

It was calm.

It was over.

Almost.

Chapter 19

Quincey Morris made a sudden strange noise and sank to the ground, clutching his chest where he had been wounded by the Gypsies.

We all jumped to him, but it was clear that he wasn't going to make it to the end of the chapter.

The strange thing was that even in his pain he was smiling. "Look," he said, pointing to Mina. "The curse is lifted. You are healthy again!"

Mina's face, so pale and thin before, was full of life, and normal, and her neck holes were healed. The evil that Dracula had done was gone.

Then Morris coughed. "Man alive . . ." he said. Then he rested his head on the ground. "I mean . . . dead."

He breathed a long breath, and it was over for him.

Quincey Morris was gone. It was definitely a bummer, but I figured that he had made it through most of the book and was a fairly cool character, so it wasn't too bad for him. Plus, he was one of the two guys who actually killed Dracula. Not bad for a Texan from Texas.

For a long time after he died no one made a sound. Then all of us—Harker, Mina, Dr. Seward, Lord Godalming, Van Helsing, Frankie, and I—looked over at the place where Dracula had been.

Finally, the professor breathed deeply and spoke. "No one will have belief of what happened here."

"It's sort of very impossible," I said.

"But we know it *did* happen," Frankie added, tapping the brown book she clutched so tightly.

At that moment, we spied something blue and flickery in the trees just beyond where we stood.

I blinked. "Frankie, is that—"

"The zapper gates!" she said. "I guess our story really is over. I can hardly believe it. . . ."

We turned to our friends.

"Thanks for the great book, you guys," I said. "But it looks as if Frankie and I need to leave now."

Mina gave us a hug. "Be watchful, always," she said.

Harker nodded. "You've been a great help."

Dr. Seward shook our hands. "There are strange things in the world. May you both travel safely."

"Thanks," said Frankie.

"No, thank *you*, for everything," Lord Godalming said. "You proved yourselves good friends to us."

Finally, Van Helsing stomped over. "Well, my youngsters two. Today a great thing you have done. Always you shall remember what happened here between us."

"I'll say!" I said. "We read a whole book!"

"Not quite," said Frankie.

"What do you mean?" I asked.

She held up the book. Between her thumb and forefinger was a single page. "We are here."

"Not . . ."

She nodded. "The last page."

"Holy cow, I want to read it!" I said, reaching for the book.

She pulled it back. "Me first! I earned it."

"No, me!"

"It's mine!"

"No, mine!"

The book flew out of our hands. We jumped after it.

KKKKKK! The whole world went blue when the book fell between the gates. Then everything went dark for a split second, and we found ourselves tumbling over and over industrial carpeting until we hit the leg of a table.

We unrolled ourselves and looked around.

"The library workroom!" Frankie shouted.

My eyes sought out the clock on the wall. "At the end of second period! And the wall's not cracked anymore. We're home! We did it! This is excellent!"

We got to our feet, stretched, breathed, and then stared at each other.

"This is so weird," said Frankie. "I feel as if we've been away forever."

"And now we're back to reality?" I said.

"Yeah." Then she shook her head. "Actually, no. Because the book seemed so real while we were in it."

I thought about that. "Maybe that's the thing with books. If you really read them, they do become real."

Just then, we heard the rapid patter of feet as they approached the workroom door.

"Mrs. Figglehopper!" I said. "Quick, back to work!"

We bounded up to the table and sat down.

The second we plunked down into our seats, Mrs. Figglehopper flung open the door and barged in.

"Well!" she boomed, as we taped up the last page and closed the back cover of *Dracula*, finished at last. "Having fun?"

It wasn't a question I had an answer to, so I gave her a look that probably made her think I was an idiot.

Frankie answered for me. "Pretty much, yeah."

"Splendid!" The librarian picked up the book and examined it. "You seem to have finished the entire book. All the pages are nicely taped. Good work."

"It wasn't as boring as we thought," I said.

"Oh, I know!" Mrs. Figglehopper said.

Now, I won't say her eyes exactly twinkled when she said that, but they were very bright.

When she left a moment later, Frankie nudged me. "Do you think she knows? I mean, about the zapper gates, and the crack in the wall, and getting into the book and all? I mean, they're her gates and her wall."

I gave a shrug of the shoulders. "Not sure," I said. "But just in case, we'd better not say anything, you know. We should probably just keep it a secret."

Frankie agreed. "It's not like anyone would believe us."

The next day in English class Frankie and I asked Mr. Wexler if we could give an oral report on *Dracula*.

"Dazzle me," he said, narrowing his eyes.

We did dazzle him. For forty minutes we talked all about our detailed knowledge of the original classic vampire saga.

We discussed theme (the awesome victory of good stuff over bad-evil stuff), setting (Transylvania, Whitby, London, then Transylvania again), and character (good husband Harker, extremely bad-evil creep-head yucky doofus vampire Dracula, poor babe Lucy, language-twisting vamp expert Van Helsing, pretty almost-vampire Mina, regular guy Dr. Seward, noble Texan Quincey Morris, fancy Lord Godalming, and garlic-snitching Mrs. Westenra). Then, while the plot mostly took place in winter, we summarized it anyway.

"It all comes down to this," I said, finally. "There are bad things in the world."

"And bad people," said Frankie, "who mostly have very long teeth, red eyes, and a big cape."

"But if you have friends helping you out, you can take on any challenge."

"Including a very fat chubby book!"

Frankie and I looked at each other. We shrugged.

"Mr. Wexler, can we sit down now?" I asked.

Our teacher gave us both the eye. It was clear he didn't understand how we could actually know so much about *Dracula*. But he couldn't prove anything.

"Oh . . . just take your seats!" he said.

But we didn't take them anywhere.

We just sat down.

Dear Reader:

Like Mr. Wexler, I, too, heard Frankie and Devin's class report about Bram Stoker's classic book, *Dracula*.

While their report shows that they must have read the book (their story is strangely close to Stoker's actual tale), I can't think how in the world they did it, can you? There simply wasn't time to read five hundred pages!

Oh, well. Never mind. Classics are classics for a reason. Once readers get "into" a good book, I find they just have to keep reading until they're done!

Still, a few words about the real author and his book might be helpful here.

Abraham "Bram" Stoker was born in Dublin, Ireland, in 1847. Listening to his mother retell the old Irish legends, little Bram's ears were filled with tales of banshees, water goblins, and child-stealing demons. No doubt these old legends fueled Bram's lifelong fascination with fantasy and terror. How nice!

After graduating from Dublin's Trinity College, Bram spent his days managing a theater and his nights writing stories and novels. None of his books was successful until, in 1890, he began work on his masterpiece.

The most famous of all vampire tales, *Dracula* is a novel told in letters, journal entries, diary excerpts, even a newspaper clipping. Bram did much research in the famous British Museum. There he learned about vampire legends, folk beliefs, and the terrain of Transylvania (now part of Romania). He must have done a good job, for he clearly scared the wits out of Frankie and Devin!

When Bram's book was published in 1897, it was instantly hailed as the finest vampire tale ever written. Over a century later, *Dracula* remains unequaled in its ability to scare the cookies out of you.

While the book is mainly about the terrible effects of evil on ordinary lives—Dracula left many victims scattered across Europe—Devin and Frankie also discovered that the book shows how friendship and love can knock the stuffing out of evil (or the dust out of a vampire!). For even though Quincey Morris dies, the novel ends with the birth of a son to Jonathan and Mina. In memory of their friend, they name the child Quincey.

By the time Bram Stoker died in 1912, he had written nineteen books. But none has been read with such fascination and fright as his classic, *Dracula*.

If you ask me, readers should wait until they are Devin and Frankie's age to read the original. You need a good vocabulary and a cheery disposition—not to mention a strong stomach. One more thing: never read a horror book at night! I found that out the hard way.

Note to self: those security gates have started buzzing again. Check it out before someone gets suspicious.

Check it out? Look at me, I've made a library joke!

Well, that's all for now. See you where the books are!

I. M. Figglehopper

Crack open the next book and take a peek at the next

#2: **Mississippi River Blues**
(*The Adventures of Tom Sawyer*)

Chapter 1

"Devin Bundy!"

No answer.

"Frankie Lang!"

No answer.

Well, no answer except maybe a stifled giggle.

You see, our English teacher, Mr. Wexler, was huffing down the halls of Palmdale Middle School looking for me and my best-friend-forever-even-though-she's-a-girl Frankie (Francine) Lang. And by the growly tone of Mr. Wexler's voice—a tone we had definitely heard before—he was roaring mad.

"When I find you two, I'll . . ."

But he wouldn't find us. Frankie and I were hiding out in the janitor's tiny supply closet among the smelliest cleaning fluids and stalest work shirts that ever burned your nostrils.

It stunk in there, but that's what made it the best hiding place. Nobody ever wanted to open that door. It could cause instant brain death to anyone who ever sniffed the air in there.

But brain death didn't bother Frankie and me.

"Wherever you are," Mr. Wexler said, "I hope you're studying for my test!"

"Studying?" I whispered to Frankie. "I don't think so. I studied for a test last year. I'm still getting over the shock to my system!"

"Tell me about it," Frankie said, nodding in agreement. "It was a one-way ticket to Headache City."

I had to laugh. I mean, everybody knows that Frankie and I aren't the best students in our class. In fact, we happen to know the best student in our class. He reads thick books all the time and he wears pants so short you can see his socks.

"I'll find you-ou-ou!" Mr. Wexler said finally. Then, rattling the lockers and pounding on the lavatory doors, he plodded away down the hall.

"Hurry, Dev," said Frankie, whipping a large square book out of her backpack and handing it to me. "We've got twelve minutes before Mr. Wexler tests us on this book. So crack it open and start reading. Unless you want to spend the rest of your life in summer school."

I shivered. "Summer . . . school. Two words that definitely don't go together! Okay, I'm reading."

I turned to the first page of the book.

On it was a picture of a smiling teddy bear wearing a cute sailor suit. He sat in a tiny boat in shallow water at the beach. "Are you sure this is the book Mr. Wexler is going to test us on?" I asked.

Frankie nodded. "*The Adventures of Timmy the Sailor*. He said it's a classic that he read five times as a kid. Now read. We have to pass this test."

"One classic coming up," I said. I began to read.

> *"Timmy the Sailor was in his boat.*
> *Timmy was happy in his boat.*
> *'Boats are fun, fun, fun!' said Timmy."*

A sudden pain shot into my head. "So many words! The story's too complicated. I can't read anymore!"

Frankie sighed. "But, Devin, what about the test?"

"If we're not there, we can't take it," I said. "I suggest we just wait here until it's over. In the meantime, I've got a neat jumbo paperclip in my pocket. We could twist it into weird shapes. What do you have?"

It was cool how I won her over.

"Well, I've got some kite string. We can play miniature rodeo!"

3

"Frankie, you are the best!" I said. "Ya—hoo!"

But at the exact moment I shouted the "hoo" part of "yahoo," I flung my arms up in joy. This action dislodged one of the janitor's smelly work shirts from its hook. This is the reason no one sets foot let alone other parts of themselves, in this closet. When this shirt fell from its hook, it settled directly onto my nose.

"Akkkk!"

I accidently breathed in the maximum amount of horrifying stink of the janitor's crusty armpit that it's possible for a human kid to breathe in.

"Ackkkkk!" I screamed again.

To keep the odor from burning my face, I ripped the shirt off and flung it away.

Right onto Frankie's nose. She let out a howl like a puppy whose paw had just been stepped on.

"EEEEOOOOOWWWW!"

She flung herself back against the door—*blam!*—it suddenly opened and hallway light flooded over us. And a face was staring at us.

"Gotcha!" boomed the voice of Mr. Wexler.

We were caught.

Again.

"So!" said our teacher, a slow grin working its way across his face. "Devin Bundy and Francine Lang. Hiding out, eh? I should send you to the office right now."

4

A glimmer of hope stirred in my brain. We couldn't take the test in the office. "You definitely should."

"But I won't," he stated. "Our test starts in nine minutes and you are going to take it." Then he sighed. "Did you even bother to read the book?"

"We did read it!" I said. I held up the book proudly. "And I know what you're thinking."

He glanced at the book. "Oh, really?"

"You're thinking, how do kids who are so over-whelmed with activities—nachos, pizza, CDs, music, homework, pony rides, church, temple, school, shop-ping, sleeping, and, of course, over four hundred cable stations—find time in their busy days to read a book?"

He stared at the book. "That's not what I'm thinking."

"Well, it's not easy," I went on. "True, we are com-pletely swamped by life. Over*booked*, you might say."

"I wouldn't."

"But the reason we read this book, Mr. Wexler, is because Frankie and I . . . believe in books—"

"That's not the book I assigned," Mr. Wexler said.

My heart did a little fluttering thing. I tapped the cover of the book and spoke words. "*The Adventures of Timmy the Sailor*. It's what you said in class."

The man breathed out loudly through his nose.

"Why would I assign a twelve-page picture book for a kindergarten reading level?"

Frankie shrugged. "To make it tough on us?"

"I did not ask you to read *The Adventures of Timmy the Sailor*," our teacher insisted. "I asked you to read *The Adventures of Tom Sawyer*! It's a three-hundred-page classic novel written by the great American author Mark Twain over a hundred and twenty-five years ago."

I looked at Frankie. She looked at me.

"Tom Sawyer?" she said.

"Yes," said the teacher.

"Not *Timmy the Sailor*?" I asked.

"No," said the teacher.

When he said that, my mind returned to its usual state. It went blank.

At this point, Mr. Wexler sucked in such a huge breath that if Frankie hadn't held onto me, I think I would have gotten sucked right up his nose.

"You—you—you—" he sputtered.

Frankie cringed. "We—we—we—what?"

"You are just not applying yourselves!" Mr. Wexler responded. "It's so—so—disappointing! If you two worked more—if you worked at all!—you really could become good students!"

Frankie jumped. "What a great idea. How about we take the test when we become good students?"

The teacher shook his head slowly, then pointed down the hall. "To class. Both of you. Now."

There was no reasoning with the guy. I had to act fast. I clutched my chest. "My heart is having appendicitis! Get me to the ER!"

I staggered down the hall to the front doors.

"Oh, no, you don't!" said Mr. Wexler, thrusting himself between me and freedom. "The only 'getting' you'll do is to be 'getting' to class, where—in eight minutes—you'll be taking my test on *Tom Sawyer*!"

"But we're not prepared!" cried Frankie.

"Be creative," the teacher said. "Stretch your minds. Dare I say it, think!"

Frankie scoffed. "Don't be ridiculous, Mr. Wexler. It's Devin and me you're talking to—"

He only grinned at that. "Come along, now. It's test time!"

Then, just when things looked darkest for us, there came a tremendous crashing sound from the end of the hallway.

Boom-da-boom!

And someone cried out.

"Help! Help me!"